INVASION OF THE BOY SNATCHERS

A CLIQUE NOVEL BY LISI HARRISON

poppy

LITTLE, BROWN AND COMPANY
New York   Boston

Poppy

Little, Brown and Company
Hachette Book Group USA
237 Park Avenue, New York, NY 10017
For more of your favorite series, go to www.pickapoppy.com

First Edition: October 2005

The Poppy name and logo are trademarks of Hachette Book Group USA

ALLOYENTERTAINMENT   Produced by Alloy Entertainment
151 West 26th Street, New York, NY 10001

ISBN-10: 0-316-70134-3 / ISBN-13: 978-0-316-70134-1

10 9 8 7
CWO
Printed in the United States of America

CLIQUE novels by Lisi Harrison:

THE CLIQUE

BEST FRIENDS FOR NEVER

REVENGE OF THE WANNABES

INVASION OF THE BOY SNATCHERS

THE PRETTY COMMITTEE STRIKES BACK

DIAL L FOR LOSER

IT'S NOT EASY BEING MEAN

SEALED WITH A DISS

And keep your eye out for BRATFEST AT TIFFANY'S—and THE CLIQUE's new look— coming February 2008.

If you like THE CLIQUE, you may also enjoy:

Bass Ackwards and Belly Up by Elizabeth Craft and Sarah Fain
Secrets of My Hollywood Life by Jen Calonita
Haters by Alisa Valdes-Rodriguez
Betwixt by Tara Bray Smith

For Bubbie Rose

"Done, done, and done." Massie Block stretched out her arms so she looked like the letter *T*, then collapsed face-first onto the fluffy purple duvet cover on her bed. Goose-down feathers puffed up around her like a taco shell when she landed, and she could feel her aching legs throbbing to the beat of her pounding heart. Who knew putting twenty-six Christmas presents away could be harder on the body than an eight-hour shopping spree on Fifth Avenue?

After a brief moment of peace, Massie's amber eyes popped open and filled with panic.

"Ehmagod, Bean, what have I done?" She beckoned to her black pug. "Now my sheets are all messy." Massie used her last bits of arm strength to push herself off the bed, and once she was standing on her white sheepskin rug, she smoothed her hand over the duvet and pulled each corner so it was taut and crease-free. She admired the gold lion charm as it dangled off her bracelet and dragged across the purple cotton. It was a Christmas gift from Claire. And Massie legitimately liked it.

"It has double meaning," Claire had said as she'd handed Massie the square-shaped red metallic box on Christmas day. "It's a Leo, 'cause that's your birth sign. And since it's a lion, like my last name, you'll always remember who gave it to you."

Massie remembered how her stomach had churned after Claire said that. It had reminded her that the Lyons were about to move to Chicago. And Claire's bright, innocent smile made it obvious that she still had no clue. Now that the holidays were over and school was about to start up again, Jay Lyons was finally going to break the news to his only daughter. Massie checked the stainless steel face of her new Coach watch with the dyed mahogany calf-hair strap. In one hour Claire would know everything.

Massie shook her head. She had worked too hard perfecting her bedroom and refused to let the Claire situation cloud the moment. There would be plenty of time for sadness later. So instead, she put her hands on her hips and admired her work.

"Bean, I don't know what gift I ah-dore more." Massie's puppy was curled up in her new doggie bunk bed, fighting to keep her tired eyes open. "My new Bean mannequin or my Glossip Girl collection? They are both so ah-mazing."

Every year for Christmas Massie got a new mannequin that had been custom made to her exact size. It was the perfect way for her to try on different outfits without having to get undressed and mess up her hair. Right now, her mannequin was wrapped in three different Dixons—the colored mesh tubes that she'd gotten as a special gift from the *Teen People* fashion editors. The gift had been their way of saying thank-you for modeling in their holiday issue. And Massie couldn't have been happier. She had already thought of thirty-seven ways to wear a Dixon and knew that with a little time she'd think of more.

But Massie wasn't the only girl with her own mannequin. This year Santa had gotten one for Bean too.

The spongy foam dog was dressed in a maroon cable-knit wool sweater, tiny beige Ugg boots, and a cashmere scarf covered in different-colored pom-poms. It was tonight's après-dinner walk ensemble. Bean had picked it out herself.

To the right of the mannequins, beside Massie's closet door, was a long mirrored shelf lined with twenty-two different tubes of lip gloss. Now that she was a member of the Glossip Girl club, a fresh exotic flavor arrived at her doorstep every morning. Candy Apple was the latest addition. And it was delicious.

Her enormous walk-in closet was stuffed with colorful stacks of cashmere sweaters that she'd bought in Aspen and four new pairs of jeans. She'd even managed to add seven new rhinestone brooches to her current collection, which brought her total up to twenty-four and pretty much guaranteed her title of Girl with the Most Brooches at Octavian Country Day School.

In a moment of sheer creative brilliance, Massie had stuck them to a red corkboard above her desk so they would sparkle over her head while she did her homework, like constellations made of jewels.

Yes, Massie was ready for the new semester.

She sat down at her desk and switched on her new Power Mac G5 computer. It was time she shared her "In" and "Out" lists with the public by turning them into a blog. What better way to help losers keep track of the latest trends? It was all part of her New Year's resolution to make the world a better place. Massie smiled to herself while the G5's hard drive booted up. She was making a difference.

The instant Massie was online, a barrage of "welcome back" instant messages popped up on her screen. She clicked on Alicia Rivera's first.

HOLAGURRL: HOW WZ ASPEN?
MASSIEKUR: GR8. AH-MAZING SNOW. HOW WZ SPAIN?
HOLAGURRL: LOCO.

Massie rolled her eyes. Every time Alicia came back from visiting her family in Spain she acted Spanish. She spoke with a Spanish accent and overused words like *loco* and *amigo*. Thankfully, by midweek she'd remember she was 100 percent American and return to normal.

HOLAGURRL: MY 13-YR-OLD COUSIN NINA CAME BACK WITH US. SHE'S GOING 2 SPEND THE SEMESTER @ OCD. WE R HAVING A WELCOME 2 WESTCHESTER FIESTA 4 HER 2MORROW NIGHT. EVERY 1 IS INVITED. BRIARWOOD BYZ 2!

Massie felt the bottoms of her feet tingle when she read, "Briarwood boys." The Briarwood Academy was known for two things: its soccer team and ah-dorable boys. And her latest crush, Derrick Harrington—or Derrington, as she secretly liked to call him—happened to be a star in both categories. And if she remembered correctly, Alicia's cousin Nina would not be a threat.

Massie had seen enough Nina pictures over the years to know that the girl was a full-fledged LBR—Loser Beyond Repair. Her clothes were totally Sears. And her hair was overprocessed and underconditioned. She looked like a "before" picture from *Extreme Makeover*.

Thankfully, Nina was one year older than Massie, so chances were their paths wouldn't cross. There was nothing worse than being seen with a dorky foreign exchange student. It was popularity poison.

Ding.

An IM from Kristen Gregory.

SEXYSPORTSBABE: HOWZ YOUR ASPEN J?
MASSIEKUR: HA HA!
SEXYSPORTSBABE: SOOO BORING HERE W/O U.
MASSIEKUR: HOW R U?
SEXYSPORTSBABE: BALD.
MASSIEKUR: ???
SEXYSPORTSBABE: MOM MADE ME GO 2 SUPER-
CUTS. THEY SCALPED ME. I'M WEARING MY
GRANDFATHER'S FEDORA. GOT ANY COOL CAPS?

MASSIEKUR: NO WAY! CAPS ARE OUT.

SEXYSPORTSBABE: SO IS LOOKING LIKE RYAN SEACREST.

MASSIEKUR: SEACREST OUT!

SEXYSPORTSBABE: SO NOT FUNNY!

Next, Massie clicked on Dylan Marvil's IM.

BIGREDHEAD: I GAINED 3 LBS OVER BREAK. AM FATTER THAN SANTA.

MASSIEKUR: ????

BIGREDHEAD: THE FOOD IN TONGA SUCKED. THE ONLY THING TO EAT ON THE ISLAND WAS FRIES W/ TARTAR SAUCE. UNLESS OF COURSE YOU LIKE FISH WITH THE HEADS STILL ON THEM.

MASSIEKUR: EW!

BIGREDHEAD: THIS YEARZ GONNA SUCK. I THINK I CAUGHT A COLD ON THE PLANE. SICK PEOPLE SHOULD NOT B ALLOWED IN 1st CLASS.

MASSIEKUR: AGREED.

BIGREDHEAD: COULD B WORSE. I COULD B CLAIRE. HOW DID SHE TAKE THE NEWS ABOUT CHICAGO?

MASSIEKUR: SHHHHH! SHE DOESN'T KNOW YET.

Massie was interrupted by Kristen's IM response.

SEXYSPORTSBABE: BTW, HOW DID CLAIRE TAKE THE NEWS?

She was interrupted again by Alicia's.

HOLAGURRL: DID CLAIRE MOVE TO CHICAGO YET?
MASSIEKUR: I'M CALLING YOU.

The three pea-sized silver bells that hung from Massie's cell phone antenna clanged together as she speed-dialed her best friends. This conversation was way too classified for IM.

"Are you insane?" Massie barked once all four girls were on the phone. "Claire could have been sitting right beside me." She looked to make sure her door was closed before continuing. "I told you never to talk about Claire and Chicago until the story goes public."

"Rorsy," Kristen whispered softly.

"*What?*" The rest of them said.

"That's a word jumble," Kristen said, as though it were obvious. "I was so bored over Christmas break I finished eleven word jumble books. I like them much better than crossword puzzles."

"Sorry!" Alicia shouted.

Massie flicked one of the bell charms with her thumb. "Huh?"

"*Rorsy* is word jumble for *sorry*," Alicia insisted.

Massie could practically hear her proud smile through the phone, her perfect white teeth gleaming and twinkling against her tanned skin.

"Wait, so does this mean Claire *still* doesn't know she's moving to Chicago?" Dylan asked.

Massie sighed. "Yup."

"On yaw!" Kristen said.

"Yes way!" Massie replied as quickly as she could. Alicia wasn't the only one who could speak jumble. "Mr. Lyons is breaking it to the families tonight at my dad's country club."

"How do you know all of this?" Dylan demanded.

"Claire's younger brother, Todd, feeds me secret information. All I had to do was buy him the new Atari Anthology. Now he tells me everything he overhears."

"No fair, I want a Todd," Alicia whined.

"*I'm* your Todd," Massie said.

"Gawd, how did you keep the secret the whole time you were in Aspen together?" Kristen asked. "You two are sooo close. I thought it would have slipped out eventually."

"It wasn't easy," Massie explained, ignoring Kristen's sarcasm. "But I didn't want to ruin her trip."

"Awww, how sweet of you," Dylan cooed insincerely. Then her tone became stern and serious. "But maybe she'd be better off in Chicago. And then things could finally get back to normal around here."

"Yeah," Kristen said.

Massie ran her fingers through her dark glossy hair and

sighed. "What are you trying to say?" she asked, even though she knew the answer.

"Nothing," Alicia said, trying to keep the peace. "They're not saying anything."

"Listen," Massie said, "the Lyonses have been living in my guesthouse since September, and it's pretty much sucked. No one knows that more than you guys. And now that Claire and I have finally decided to stop making each other miserable, you're all upset. I don't get it. I thought you'd be happy for me."

"We're glad you're not making each other miserable, but did you have to become BFFs?" Dylan said, and then blew her nose.

It was obvious Kristen, Dylan, and Alicia were jealous. And Massie wasn't in the mood to deal. She took a deep breath and, when she exhaled, let all of her friend-stress go. The last few months had been so full of fighting, and Massie desperately wanted the new year to be fun.

She heard a light tapping on her bedroom door. "Gotta go," she whispered.

"Was it something we said?" Alicia sounded genuinely concerned.

"No. Claire's here."

"Shocker," Dylan said under her breath.

"She's always there," Kristen said before hanging up.

Massie snapped her phone shut and quickly shut off her computer. "Come in."

Claire pushed the door open but stayed in the hallway. She widened her big blue eyes and opened her mouth. She looked like a shocked emoticon. "I can't believe my eyes."

"Me either," Massie said to Claire's shoes. "Are you really wearing *those* to the High Hills Country Club tonight?"

"I thought you'd like my new camo high-tops." Claire stuck out her right leg and pointed her toes like a ballerina. "They're Converse, not Keds."

"I know what they are." Massie raised her eyes, scanning Claire's faded high-waisted Gap jeans and then her flower-print button-down with pink pearl western buttons.

"I knew you'd like them." Claire smiled. "I e-mailed a picture of them to Cam and he said he got the exact same pair over break. I swear sometimes I think we're more like twins than boyfriend and girlfriend."

"So, are you and Cam Fisher officially boyfriend and girlfriend now?" Massie asked casually. She didn't want Claire to know how much that news shocked her. But how could it not? Claire actually had a real boyfriend before she did. That was not supposed to happen.

"Yeah, he just asked me." Claire blushed. "It was so cute—he sent me an Evite inviting me to be his girlfriend."

Massie pretended to be distracted by a piece of lint on the sleeve of her tweed blazer.

Claire giggled softly, then said, "I RSVP'd 'yes.'"

Massie looked up. "That's great." She forced herself to

smile. "But that still doesn't change the fact that you're planning to wear camo sneakers to a country club."

Claire rolled her eyes and smiled.

Massie was tempted to say she wouldn't use those shoes to scoop up Bean's poo. But she couldn't be mean. Not tonight.

"Your room looks ah-mazing." Claire changed the subject. Massie giggled when she heard Claire using one of her expressions. After all, imitation is the sincerest form of flattery.

"Thanks. Wanna see all my new clothes?" Massie waved her arms in the air like a game-show hostess.

"Uh, sure." But she was staring at Massie's Glossip Girl collection.

"Feel free to wear whatever you want to the club tonight." Massie pushed her closet door and it popped open. She tugged on the purple feather boa that hung from the light switch in the middle of the ceiling and a warm orange light lit the inside, triggering a disco ball that automatically started spinning, sending white, swirling squares across the walls.

"It looks like Benetton in here." Claire admired the colorful selection.

"More like Bergdorf's. Here." Massie yanked a caramel-colored cashmere cowl-neck sweater off a hanger and draped it over Claire's shoulder. Then she grabbed her dark Juicy Couture jeans and a pair of two-inch teal round-toe Marc Jacobs boots. "Wear this. And cuff the jeans so the boots show."

"Why are you letting me wear your new clothes?"

"The club has a dress code."

Claire held the jeans in her arms and crinkled her eyebrows. "What is it?"

"Cool," Massie said with a playful smile.

Claire giggled and shrugged.

Before she slid off her jeans, Claire emptied her pockets. "Want one?" She dangled a clear plastic bag in front of Massie's face. Tangles of oily gummy worms were stuck together in a sweaty clump.

"Uh, okay," Massie said, making every effort to be nice.

"Really?" Claire pulled the bag away. "But you hate sugar."

"No, I don't," Massie said, reaching for it. "Remember all of those mints I stole from the front desk at the ski lodge?"

The girls started cracking up when they remembered how stuffed Massie's pockets had been. She'd barely been able to walk.

"Yeah, but you didn't eat those; we threw them off the chair lifts." Claire laughed.

"I ate a few." Massie dug her hand into the bag. It was humid inside. She wouldn't have felt any more disgusted if the worms had been real.

"Oh, here." Claire tossed her digital camera to Massie.

"What's this camera for?"

"I thought we could download the pictures from our trip onto your new computer." Claire fell backward onto Massie's bed. She was struggling to fasten the jeans.

"Uh, can you . . . ?" Massie was about to ask Claire to get off her bed, but it was too late. The duvet was already dented.

"I thought we could e-mail the good ones to Cam." Claire sounded like she had just been punched in the stomach, until she finally closed the jeans. "I want to show him what a good time we had in Aspen. We should send some to Derrington too."

Massie's stomach flip-flopped when she heard Derrington's name. No matter how hard she tried, she hadn't been able to stop thinking about Derrington over break, and she wondered if he missed her half as much. He'd popped into her head as she was opening presents on Christmas day and while she was skiing moguls in Aspen. Massie had no idea why she was crushing so hard on a guy who wore shorts in the winter and insisted on wiggling his bare butt in public at least three times a week. Yes, his shaggy blond hair and sparkly brown eyes made him cuter than the majority of the Briarwood boys, and yes, he was the most valued player on their soccer team, but it was more than that. It had something to do with the fact that he'd exchanged the Diesel jeans Massie had bought him for Christmas and gotten two pairs of cargo shorts instead. On one hand it was rude, but on the other it was kind of cool. Derrington was the only person Massie had ever met who wasn't afraid of her. And that made Massie a little afraid of him, in a good way. "I'll need time to Photoshop them. I'm not sending anything unless we look ah-mazing."

"Fine with me," Claire agreed as she pulled the cowl-neck sweater over her head.

Kendra Block's pinched voice bleated over the white intercom on Massie's bedside table.

"Girls, we're leaving for the club in five minutes," she said.

"'Kay, Mom," Massie yelled to the white box.

"I wonder what my dad's big surprise is." Claire smiled and bit her bottom lip. She leaned against Massie's desk and slid on the teal boots. Her face looked like it was being swallowed by the wide cowl-neck as she looked down to zip them up. "I bet he wants to celebrate my first A ever in Spanish. Or maybe we're finally trading in that Ford Taurus for a new car."

Claire hobbled around Massie's room, trying to get her balance in Massie's heels. "Wait, I know—I bet they're buying a ski house in Aspen right next to yours so we can go there together every Christmas. How awesome would that be?" The excitement made Claire lose her balance. She teetered for a few seconds and then fell face-first into the butt of the Bean mannequin, which then knocked over the Massie mannequin. They both came crashing down on top of Claire. In an instant she was buried under a tangle of spongy arms, legs, and paws.

"Ehmagod, are you okay?" Massie was glad Claire couldn't see the smile that was fighting its way onto her face.

A muffled "ugggh" was all she heard back.

Massie started laughing so hard she couldn't breathe. Then tears welled up in her eyes. And before she knew it, her teeth were chattering and she was crying, for real.

Claire pulled herself out from under the heap of body parts. Her torso was shaking with laughter and her otherwise pale cheeks were flushed.

When she finally caught her breath, Claire looked at Massie with a trace of concern. "Are you crying? Because if anyone gets to cry, it should be me." She rubbed her elbow.

"No." Massie wiped her cheeks. "I just get teary when I laugh too hard." It wasn't entirely true, but it was a lot cooler than saying, "I am crying because you're the closest thing I've ever had to a sister and I hate that you have to leave."

"Sorry about the mannequins. I don't think they're broken." Claire pulled off the teal boots and slid on her camo high-tops.

While Claire laced up, Massie double-checked her own outfit. Her new True Religion jeans fit perfectly and the chocolate-brown tweed blazer with the velvet rope belt was perfect for the club. But it needed a little extra something. Massie climbed up on her desk and reached for the red corkboard on her ceiling. She plucked the green four-leaf clover brooch out of the cork and forced the pin through the thick tweed on her lapel. She needed all the luck she could get.

"Ow!" she yelped.

"What?"

"I pricked myself." Massie watched a ruby red bead of blood ooze out onto her finger. She waved her left hand in the air to shake off the sting.

"Does it hurt?" Claire asked. "Do you need a Band-Aid?"

Massie sucked on her throbbing thumb, thinking about what lay ahead. "Nah, it's nothing." The rest of her night was going to hurt a lot more.

Before Claire Lyons moved to Westchester, the closest she had ever come to a ritzy country club was the newly renovated Orlando YMCA.

Now she was standing under a massive glittery chandelier in the round foyer of the main dining room in the High Hills Country Club, surrounded by vases full of long-stemmed red roses. The rich, sweet smell of buttery steak sizzling in the kitchen was so mouthwatering, Claire knew her days of being impressed by the Y's double cheeseburger were behind her forever.

A clean-shaven middle-aged man in a stiff tuxedo grabbed a stack of heavy red velvet menus off the hostess stand. "Right this way, Mr. Block." He nodded, then led the two families through the crowded but quiet dining room.

Todd, Claire's ten-year-old brother, was clinging to Massie's side even more than usual, and Claire wondered why Massie was tolerating it. Usually she found a way to shake him. But tonight it actually seemed like they were in cahoots, exchanging knowing glances. For a minute Claire found herself wondering if Massie's body had been possessed by a rare breed of aliens that appreciated red-headed brats.

"What's going on with you two?" Claire asked. "Do I have a booger or something?" She wiped her hand across her nose.

"No, everything is fine," said Massie. Her amber eyes weren't flickering like they usually did.

"You sure?" Claire asked.

"Fully." Massie opened her brown leather clutch and began searching it with a sense of urgency. But Claire knew Massie was really just looking for something to say. She just didn't know why.

They snaked around the tables in an uncomfortable silence until they heard, "BRAAACK."

It sounded like a duck's quack, but it was Todd burping. Claire instantly forgot her suspicions and burst out laughing. Her parents, Jay and Judi, whipped their heads around and glared at their kids. Kendra and William Block kept their eyes fixed on the floor-to-ceiling windows across the room, like they hadn't heard a thing.

"'Scuse me." Todd shrugged.

Massie attempted to cover her smirk with her hand, but her shaking shoulders gave her away. Claire smiled. She loved it when Massie lost control, and wanted to see more. She started gulping air.

"HIGHHILLSCOUNTRYCLUUUUB," Claire burped in Massie's ear.

Massie let out a loud cackle that instantly overpowered the delicate clanking sounds of the club's monogrammed silverware.

Todd high-fived his sister. "Ni-ice."

"That's enough!" Kendra hissed out of the side of her mouth. She pinched the ends of the fox collar on her blazer so that it hugged her long thin neck.

Claire looked at her own mother's outfit and rolled her eyes. Judi's thin black J.Crew V-necked sweater was covered in specks of white lint and random mousy brown hairs.

"I hope this table is suitable, Mr. Block." The host gestured as he pulled a cushy blue velvet chair out for Kendra.

"It's perfect, Nivens." William straightened his gold tie. "Thank you."

"Yeah, thanks, buddy," Jay Lyons said. He was wearing a wrinkled blue dinner jacket with a plaid flannel shirt underneath. Claire couldn't believe the two dads were actually friends.

Once everyone was seated around the table and their wines and Shirley Temples had been delivered, William raised his glass. Everyone followed.

"To my dear friends and neighbors." He lifted his arm a little higher. "Now Jay, will you please tell us what this big surprise is? Kendra and I are so tired of guessing."

Everyone chuckled except Massie. She was looking down at her lap, pushing back her cuticles with the yellow plastic sword that had come in her fruity mocktail. Claire wiggled forward in her seat. Was it going to be the house in Aspen or a new car?

"I don't want to move to Chicago!" Todd screamed. His face was flushed and his big brown eyes were filling up with tears.

Massie's head shot up and she punched the side of his arm.

"Massie!" Kendra gripped her silver butter knife and pressed it firmly against the table.

"Todd, what are you talking about?" Jay asked his son. But Claire didn't like her father's tone. It was laced with suspicion, not concern.

"I—hic!—know." Todd started hiccupping and crying at the same time. "Hic! We're moving to Ch—hic!—ago, and I don't wanna g—hic!—oh."

"Have you been eavesdropping again?" Judi snapped.

"Wait. Stop." Claire held out her palm in an effort to slow things down so she could jump into the conversation. "What is he talking about?"

Her parents took deep breaths but never seemed to exhale. Kendra Block twisted her princess-cut Tiffany diamond ring around on her fourth finger. William unbuttoned his suit jacket, put his elbows on the table, and folded his hands. Claire could see his knuckles turning white. Massie was biting her bottom lip and buffing her French manicure.

Claire turned to face Massie. "Do you know what they're talking about?"

Massie's cheeks turned red but she didn't look up.

"Do you?" Claire's voice cracked. She pushed Massie's arm as if she were trying to wake her out of a deep sleep. "*Do you?*"

"Claire, keep your voice down," Judi insisted, leaning forward.

"Will everyone please calm down?" Jay whispered. "This is a good thing." His smile seemed forced. "I got a great job offer in Chicago, and I've decided to take it."

"What?" Kendra snapped. William gently rested his hand on her arm. She covered her mouth with a cream-colored cloth napkin and shook her head.

"Kids, I found a four-bedroom house with enough room in the backyard for a hot tub. And you can walk to school. How great will that be?"

"Are you serious?" Claire screeched. "Are you seriously serious?" She could feel her throat starting to lock. The tears were on their way. "I'm finally having fun here and now you want me to leave?"

Claire thought of Massie's exclusive Friday-night sleep-overs that she was finally invited to. And the new friend-ships she had with Layne, Dylan, Kristen, and Alicia. Then her boyfriend Cam's ah-dorably sweet face popped into her mind. Her hands felt itchy and clammy. This couldn't possibly be happening.

Claire looked to Massie for support. She got nothing but her profile.

"Why are you so quiet?"

Massie managed to sneak a peek at Todd through the corner of her eye, without moving her head.

"No way," Claire cried. "You already knew? He told you?"

"Son, you're grounded," Jay said.

Todd pushed his plate of crusty French bread into the middle of the table. "As of now—hic!—Todd Lyons is on a hunger strike. If we leave I—hic!—am *never*—hic!—eating again."

"I'm not leaving." Claire slammed her fist on the table, and her father's glass of red wine fell on its side. A stream of bloodred liquid rushed toward Claire and doused the front of her camel-colored sweater.

"Oh my God, Massie, I'm so sorry," Claire said to the stain on Massie's sweater. The tears in her eyes made everything look blurry. "But you should have told me. This wouldn't have happened if you told me." She wiped her eyes.

"Sorry," Massie muttered under her breath.

"Ready to order, Monsieur?" the enthusiastic young waiter asked, ignoring everyone's tears.

"*Nothing* for me, thanks!" Todd shouted at the waiter. He kicked his chair away from the table and ran toward the bathroom.

"All I want is a stable childhood," Claire said to no one in particular.

"Uh, maybe we should just leave and order a coupla pizzas at home," Jay quietly suggested to William.

William nervously ran his hand across the top of his smooth bald head, then chuckled and glanced at the waiter. "That's not a bad idea." He reached into his pants pocket and peeled three crisp bills out of his wallet. "Sorry, Franco." He stuffed the bills in the waiter's jacket. "We've just received some tragic news."

Franco clasped his hands behind his back. "Understood, Mr. Block."

"I'll go get Todd," Judi sighed.

"I'll go with you," Kendra said.

Both families stood up from the table.

Claire's eyes felt swollen and heavy. And her body ached like it did when she had a fever. She had to get out of there. Suddenly, Claire turned and stormed through the dining room, wiping her eyes with one of the clubs precious cream cloth napkins. She didn't care if every rich snooty country club member was staring at her over the tops of their Chanel bifocals. At the moment, they seemed like insignificant extras in the horror movie that was her life.

Claire could hear the charms on Massie's bracelet jingling behind her as she raced to catch up. But Claire refused to slow down. She bolted straight through the round foyer and past the red roses that had once looked so cheery. Now she wished she could knock them over and hurl the crystal vases at her father's selfish head. A friendly old man held the glass doors open for Claire and she marched past him without even a single "thank-you."

No one said a word while they stood outside under the heat lamps waiting for their cars. Finally, the valets pulled up with the Blocks' Bentley and the Lyonses' Ford Taurus.

"Dad, can Claire ride in our car?" Massie asked.

"No," Jay answered for William. "She's coming with us."

"I'm walking," Claire muffled though her tears. The

thought of being anywhere near her father made her nauseated. She could hardly look at him.

"Me too," Todd added.

"*Get in the car,*" Jay insisted.

"I hate you," Claire said to the beige car door as she yanked it open.

Once they were all inside, Jay fixed his eyes on the road ahead. "Can we please talk about this?"

Claire and Todd were silent.

"Fine," Jay said. He turned the key, started the car, and drove toward the club gates.

The rhythmic clicking of the turn signal was the only noise in the car. It sounded louder than usual and seemed to be laughing at them.

Click-click-click.

Click-click-click.

Click-click-click.

Chi-ca-go.

Chi-ca-go.

Chi-ca-go.

Claire started chewing on the fingernails she'd spent all of Christmas break trying to grow. What was she supposed to do next? All she could do was glare at the back of her father's head and plan her escape. She'd uprooted her life once for him, and it had been hell. For three months straight Claire had gotten picked on by Massie and the rest of her so-called Pretty Committee. They'd put red paint on her white pants, thrown smoked salmon at her, and written mean text messages about her clothes, her bangs, and her only friend, Layne. Now that she finally fit in, she wasn't about to leave and start all over again.

Bzzzz, bzzzz, bzzzz. Claire felt something vibrating against her hip. She immediately unzipped the inside pocket of her ski jacket and pulled out her cell phone.

"What is that?" Judi asked.

Bzzzz, bzzzz, bzzzz.

Claire quickly sat on the phone. "Uh." She looked at Todd, desperate for a quick cover-up. If her parents found out Massie had bought her a cell phone for Christmas, they would take it away. For some reason, they expected her to wait until her sixteenth birthday before she could enter modern civilization.

"Sorry, I farted," Todd announced.

Judi rolled her eyes and turned around.

"Thanks," Claire mouthed to her brother.

Todd winked. When the vibrating stopped, Claire picked up the phone and turned the ringer to silent. Then she shoved it under her coat and discreetly checked the screen. She had one text message.

MASSIE: Don't worry, my dad will figure something out.
CLAIRE: ?
MASSIE: He is talking 2 my mom about it now. She is crying.
CLAIRE: Me 2.

MASSIE: ☹
CLAIRE: HLP.
MASSIE: Trying . . . C U at home.

Claire sighed. She stuffed her phone back inside her jacket and prayed for a miracle.

Jay flicked the turn signal again and followed the Blocks' Bentley into their circular driveway. Claire leaned her head against the window and looked at the stone mansion. For some reason, it looked different than it had when the Lyonses had first arrived from Orlando over Labor Day weekend. It still resembled an old English manor, and it still had a huge green lawn behind it with a horse barn, swimming pool, and tennis courts. Even the stone guesthouse was the same. But over time the hard edges seemed to have softened and warmed. And the estate no longer looked ominous or intimidating. It just looked like a home. Her home.

Jay turned off the engine. The air felt heavy and still.

"Can we talk about this calmly?" Jay asked. His leather jacket made a crunching sound as turned to face the backseat.

"No," Judi, Todd, and Claire answered.

He shook his head. "Impossible," Jay muttered under his breath as he pushed open the car door and stepped onto the Blocks' gravel driveway. The tiny rocks seemed to groan as Jay carelessly trod across them in his Rockport walking shoes. Claire knew exactly how they felt.

William was there, waiting for him.

"Jay, how about we go in my study and talk about this." He closed the car door for him.

Claire listened for her father's response. *Please say yes, please say yes, please say yes. . . .*

"William, I'm not going to change my mind. This is a great opportunity and—"

"Then let's have a glass of port and you can tell me all about it." William gently nudged Jay toward the front steps of the main house.

Jay sighed, and a huge cloud of steam puffed out of his mouth. Then he turned and followed William.

Claire crossed her fingers for luck and stepped out of the car.

Twenty minutes later everyone was sitting on the cold marble floor outside William's study, dressed in their pajamas and eating pizza out of the box. Kendra sat above them on one of her toile dining room chairs, nibbling on crudités and hummus.

"I can't believe you kids are eating on the floor. You're like a pack of wild animals," she whispered. "Judi, are you sure I can't get you a chair?"

"Shhh," everyone hissed. Their ears were pressed against the tall wood doors.

"Todd, honey, please eat something." Judi pushed the half-empty box toward her son. "Starving yourself isn't going to change your father's mind."

Todd folded his arms across his chest and looked away.

Judi probably thought he was being stubborn, but Claire could tell by the patch of grease on the front of his gray Briarwood sweatshirt that he had a slice or two tucked away for later.

"I have to go to the bathroom." Todd turned his oily body away from his mother as he tried to stand.

When he came back ten minutes later, his lips were shiny and he was wearing a different sweatshirt. But the mothers didn't notice. They were too busy trying to figure out how they were going to survive without each other.

"I can't start over again," Claire sniffled. "I can't do it." A tear rolled down her cheek and dangled off her chin. She shook her head and watched it land on her Strawberry Shortcake pajama bottoms.

"Don't give up yet. My dad promised he would fix this."

"But what if he can't?" Claire whispered.

"I always get what I want," Massie assured her.

Massie wants me, Claire thought. She felt the sudden urge to throw her arms around her friend and never let go. But she didn't have to. Massie hugged her first.

Claire felt something sharp poking her in the back. She opened her eyes and lifted her head off the cold hard floor. The corner of the study door was pressing into her spine.

"Owww." She pushed herself up and crossed her legs.

"Sorry," Jay whispered as he stepped over her. "I had no idea I was walking into a stakeout."

Claire started to smile. She stopped herself when she remembered she was mad at him.

Massie, Todd, and Judi were still asleep on the floor. Kendra's head was leaning against the back of the chair. Her eyes were shut but her mouth was wide open.

William clapped his hands and everyone opened their eyes. "It's two in the morning."

Claire looked at his face for some indication of what had been said over the last five hours, but he just looked pale and tired. His blue eyes were bloodshot, and specks of stubble were sprouting up all over his face. She had never seen him look this messy. Jay looked just as disheveled, but Claire was used to seeing her father like that.

"So?" Massie jumped to her feet.

Claire rearranged her long bangs and smoothed the back of her hair. She wondered how Massie still managed to look pretty after sleeping on the floor.

"Why don't we go into the kitchen?" William suggested. "I could use some dinner."

"Just tell us now," Massie begged. "Please."

"The kitchen," William insisted.

Everyone followed the fathers. Claire, Massie, and Todd hopped up on the three stools by the counter and the parents sat at the breakfast table. They immediately focused on the Ashanti video playing on the flat-screen TV that had been built into the Blocks' refrigerator door until Kendra shut it off.

"Would you like me to fix you something to eat?" Kendra asked the dads.

They nodded, too exhausted to speak.

Kendra stood up and walked over to the microwave. She pushed it aside and spoke into the small white box behind it.

"Inez, could you please come to the kitchen?" Kendra had to ask three times before she got an answer.

"Certainly, Mrs. Block," a groggy voice finally answered back.

Inez shuffled into the kitchen wearing fuzzy slippers and a bright floral-print robe. She washed her hands and started pulling out pots and pans.

"A simple sandwich will do." William gave her an understanding smile.

"Of course." Inez nodded

"Daaa-aaad," Massie whined. "Tell us already."

William rubbed his eyes. "I think Jay should be the one to tell you."

Claire wished she could hit a button on a remote control and press Pause so she could live in this moment forever. The next few seconds held possibilities that were too scary to imagine.

Jay inhaled deeply and put his head in his hands. "We're still moving."

"What?" Claire shouted. "No!" The tears came immediately.

"Dad!" Massie wailed. "You said—"

"Let him finish," William insisted.

"We're moving out of the guesthouse for a couple of weeks so we can give it an extreme makeover." He looked at his wife with a proud smile on his face.

"What?" Judi asked.

"William offered me a big raise and a promotion and told us we can renovate the guesthouse."

Kendra looked shocked.

"You always said you wanted to remodel, dear." William put his arm around his wife.

"Kendra, we can work on it together." Judi's eyes lit up.

Kendra smiled and clapped her hands. "Winter project!" she squealed with joy.

Massie, Claire, and Todd jumped off their stools and hugged each other. They were bouncing up and down screaming, "Yay!"

Claire immediately thought of Cam. She wished he were there too. A wave of relief washed through her entire body and she started crying even harder than before. But these were tears of joy.

Inez slid two multigrain BLTs in front of the dads and managed to sneak out of the kitchen without being noticed.

"Where are we going to live while we renovate?" Judi asked.

"In a nearby motel," Jay put in.

William opened his mouth as wide as he could and prepared to take a bite of the triple-decker sandwich.

"Nonsense." Kendra shook her head. "They will move in with us until construction is done."

William froze, the sandwich inches away from his lips.

"Oh, relax, William. It will only be for a few weeks. No one works faster than the Daley brothers."

"Yes!" Todd sounded like he'd just doubled his score in Underground 2. He leaned into Claire as he whispered in her ear, "I am finally going to see Massie Block in her underwear."

"Shhh." Claire didn't want to miss a second of her parents' conversation.

"I am so going online and ordering spy gear."

"Don't you dare," Claire hissed. "I'll tell Dad."

"That's fine." Todd nodded. "We can tell him about your cell phone at the same time."

Claire folded her arms across her chest and turned to face her parents.

"Todd, you can have the guest room next to Massie's," Kendra said.

"Awesome! Thanks, Kendra," he said with a devious smile.

"Jay and Judi, you can take the upstairs room in the attic," she continued. "And since Inez has the downstairs room, Claire will have to share with Massie."

"Yayyy!" Claire cheered. "Thanks, everyone." She ran around the kitchen hugging and kissing the parents. "This is going to be so much fun." Things had turned out even better than she could have ever imagined. Sharing a room with Massie would be like Aspen all over again. They could stay up all night talking about Cam and Derrington, and they'd have even more inside jokes than they already did. This was definitely going to be a great year. She kissed her father twice on the forehead and hugged him as hard as she could.

"I love you." Claire beamed.

"Sure, now you do." Jay chuckled.

Claire turned to Massie and held out her arms. "How ah-mazing is this going to be?"

"Amazing," Massie said calmly. And then her smile faded away completely.

"Is this really Alicia's house?" Claire asked Massie as they climbed the stone steps that led to the arched mahogany door. She froze when she saw the cast-iron gargoyle knocker. "This seems like the kind of place that would have a drawbridge and fire-breathing dragons."

"Wait until you see the inside."

A deeply tanned butler wrapped in a full-length brown fur coat was positioned outside in the cold, welcoming guests to the Rivera home.

"Names, please," he said to a stack of papers on his clipboard.

"Hey, Alvie." Massie pushed past him.

"Oh, hello, Miss Block." He lifted his head. "And this is?"

"Claire Lyons. She's with me."

"Very well." Alvie lowered his clipboard. He extended his white-gloved hand toward the brass knob and pushed the door open, giving way to what looked like the inside of a Manhattan art gallery. "Coat check is beside the restrooms." He eyed the red distressed-leather sack Massie was dragging across the floor.

"Thanks, Al."

A thin neat man with slicked-back gray hair hurried

toward Massie, pinching a white plastic tag between his thumb and index finger.

"I'll take that for you," he insisted.

And just like that, her bag was gone.

The Riveras always had their parties in the front foyer because it was the only space on the estate that wasn't packed with expensive antique furniture. But the room was hardly empty.

The ceilings were so high, Massie had to tilt her head all the way back if she wanted to admire the colorful stained-glass dome ceiling. Enormous walls peppered with hundreds of oil paintings in ornate gold frames never failed to impress parents, but Massie preferred the collection of freaky Oriental masks mounted between them. No matter where she moved, their hollow eyes seemed to follow her.

A pack of young kids were chasing each other up and down the long spiral staircase that punctured the center of the room. The shape reminded Massie of a giant version of the corkscrew that Franco, the waiter at the club, used to open her father's wine. The brass banister was wrapped in red and yellow streamers, probably meant to represent the Spanish flag, and a banner that spelled out CUMPLIMENTAR, NINA in silver glitter hung off of it.

Waitresses were offering guests silver trays filled with tapas while waiters doled out alcohol-free sangria. Hundreds of orange candles filled the room with a warm glow, their flames flickering to the beat of wild flamenco music.

"How come you never had a welcome party for me?" Claire asked Massie. She slipped off her baby blue ski jacket and handed it to a teenager dressed in a black-and-white maid's outfit.

"Because you weren't welcome." Massie smiled.

Claire gave Massie a playful shove.

"Watch the outfit." Massie adjusted the white faux-fur shrug that was tied around her shoulders and made sure her black cat rhinestone brooch was still positioned just below her neckline. "This is the first time I'm seeing Derrington in weeks. I have to be a ten."

"You are," Claire gushed. "That green satin dress looks ah-mazing on you."

"It's chiffon." Massie checked for wrinkles that might have formed in the car. "Do you like my hair crimped? Or does it look like I got my head stuck in an accordion?"

"I told you, I love it." Claire ran her fingers over the jagged chunks of hair that zigzagged around Massie's face. "You're going to start a new trend tonight, I can smell it." She sniffed the air.

Massie giggled.

Before their trip to Aspen, Massie never would have shown Claire her insecure side. But these days, they spent more time together than real sisters, and it was exhausting trying to act confident 24/7. Besides, Massie knew Claire wasn't the type to hold it against her.

"Do you think Derrington is going to like it?" Massie

whispered as they inched their way into the crowd of seventh graders and parents.

"There's only one way to find out." Claire was pointing to the bottom of the staircase. "There they are." She grabbed Massie's arm and started pulling her toward the tight cluster of Briarwood boys that were hovering over Derrington and his silver Game Boy.

He was sitting on the third step of the corkscrew staircase, surrounded by his soccer buddies, Cam Fisher, Chris Plovert, and some preppy new kid Massie had never seen before. His elbows were resting on his bare kneecaps, but his thumbs and wrists were working overtime. Derrington was so involved in the game, he had to use his shoulder to brush the floppy blond strands away from his eyes. His outfit was the same as usual—cargo shorts and hiking boots. The only difference was the gray blazer and black tie he wore over his T-shirt. Overall, he looked even cuter than he had before break, like he had been exfoliated and spit-shined.

Suddenly, Massie felt weak and tingly, like all the cells in her body had turned into Diet Coke bubbles and were trapped just below the surface of her skin.

"Stop tugging on me." She pulled her arm away from Claire and placed it firmly on her hip.

"What's wrong?" Claire asked. The confident smile on her face seemed to mock Massie and her paralyzing fear. "Don't you want to say hi?"

Of course that was what Massie wanted more than anything. She had been waiting three gruelingly long weeks to see Derrington again. But now was not the time. She was totally unprepared. What would she say to him, especially with all of his friends around? And more importantly, what was her hair doing?

"Be cool, Kuh-laire," Massie whispered. "When it comes to boys, it's better to act curious, not interested." She instantly regretted wearing chiffon. When there was sweat on her body, chiffon always found it.

"But Cam already knows I'm *interested*. And Derrington knows you like him. You e-mail each other all the time."

Massie shifted her shrug to make sure it covered the pit stains that were forming under her arms.

"That was *last* year." Massie rubbed her newest Glossip Girl flavor across her lips. "It's a new year now, and they may have found other girls."

"Who's eating a sugar doughnut?" Dylan asked as she forced herself between Claire and Massie.

The three girls squealed when they saw each other. Dylan held out her arms in preparation for a giant hug. But Massie stood tall and stayed stiff, her hands pressed against her thighs. If anyone saw her sweaty pits, she'd have to transfer schools. Dylan must have sensed Massie's hesitation, because she turned and hugged Claire instead.

When she released Claire, Dylan leaned in and sniffed Massie's face. "Are those your lips I smell?"

"It's my new gloss." Massie took the shiny mirrored tube

out of her clutch and waved it in front of Dylan. "It's called Krispy Kreme. It arrived yesterday."

"It's strong." Dylan tucked a bright red curl behind her ear. "I can actually smell it through my stuffed-up nose." She coughed.

"Ew, cover your mouth." Massie laughed and fanned the air.

"Admit it." Dylan took a step back. "You're just embarrassed to be seen with me because I'm fat."

"Fat?" Claire gasped. "We're, like, the exact same size."

"I wish." Dylan inspected Claire's small round butt.

"Dylan, are you full of garbage?" Massie asked.

Dylan tugged on her dark green silk caftan. "No."

"Then why are you acting like a Hefty?"

Claire threw her head back and laughed louder than she needed to. Massie crinkled her eyebrows. She knew her joke was clever, but she didn't think it was LOL-worthy.

Massie shot Claire a What's-so-funny? look. But Claire was too busy slapping her thigh and peeking at Cam out of the corner of her eye to notice.

"Brilliant!" Massie was instantly impressed by Claire's I'm-gonna-show-Cam-how-much-fun-I-am strategy and joined in the laughter. Derrington pushed his shaggy blond hair away from his eyes and looked straight at them. Mission accomplished. Claire seemed to know more about attracting boys than J.Lo.

"Are you two laughing at me?" Dylan sniffled. "Weight problems are not something to make light of."

"Literally." Massie and Claire broke into another fit of exaggerated laughter.

"What's so funny?" They were too busy fake-laughing to notice someone had joined their circle.

Massie was just about to tell the strange boy in the black fedora to mind his own business when she heard his phlegmy laugh. He was Kristen.

Massie slapped her hand against her heart. "Ehmagod."

"I know," Kristen groaned.

"Lemme see." Massie lifted the fedora. "I'm sure it's not *that* bad." But Kristen slapped her hand away.

"Ouch," Massie snapped.

Dylan giggled into her palm, and Claire exploded into another fit of hysterical laughter.

"It's not funny, okay?" Kristen whined. "I look like a yob!"

Dylan and Claire looked at each other in utter confusion.

"Boy," Massie mouthed to them.

"Oh," they mouthed back.

"I had to steal this hat from my grandfather," Kristen confessed. "He spent twenty minutes looking for it after dinner last night, and now my grandmother is making him go to the doctor because she's convinced he's losing his mind."

"What about that lace dress?" Massie asked. "Did you steal it from your grandmother?"

"No." Kristen stomped her foot. "I'm just trying to look like a girl."

"Well, I brought the hats you asked for," Massie assured her. "They're in coat check."

"Thanks." Kristen's hardened expression softened.

Massie caught a whiff of Angel perfume and whipped her head around.

"I thought I smelled you." She turned toward Alicia.

The raven-haired beauty was standing just outside their tight cluster, holding a silver tray covered in name tags and markers. The chunky turquoise necklace around her neck and her cream-colored satin dress popped against her deep tan.

"You look ah-mazing," Dylan gushed.

"I love your hair. It's so gnol."

"Long," Massie translated.

"You think?" Alicia widened her dark brown eyes and ran her manicured fingers through the top of her shiny blowout. Her hair seemed to sway back and forth in slow motion before it settled back in position, and Massie felt like she was watching a Pantene commercial. If only Alicia would get a zit or braces or something, she'd be a little easier to look at. As it stood, her face was so perfect, it hurt to focus on it for more than a few seconds at a time. It was like looking straight into one of the UV bulbs at Sun of a Beach tanning salon.

"Did you lose weight?" Dylan asked.

"No." Alicia looked at her stomach to double-check. "I don't think so."

"Maybe your boobs got bigger," Dylan suggested.

Alicia lifted the tray so it covered her chest. "Ew, Gawd forbid."

Massie tugged on her crimped hair, wishing she hadn't picked the first party of the year to experiment. Not that anyone was even noticing.

"Where's Olivia?" Claire asked.

"She has mono." Alicia looked down at the markers on her tray.

"Boob job," Massie coughed.

Everyone laughed except Alicia. She rolled her eyes, raised her tiny nose toward the stained-glass ceiling, and kept it there until the laughter died. Massie still couldn't understand why her best friend liked Faux-livia so much, but she knew better than to ask. Ever since Alicia had tried to start her own clique, Massie had been extra careful not to do anything that might push her away again. She couldn't stand the thought of wasting another semester fighting with her friends, especially when there were so many losers to pick on.

"Have you guys seen the new Briarwood boy yet?" Alicia whispered. "He is ah-dorable."

"Am I a vampire?" Massie asked.

"Huh?" Alicia asked.

"Then why are you keeping me in the dark?" Massie asked. "Details, please."

"His name is Josh Hotz. He's a 'transfer student' from Hotchkiss." Alicia made air quotes when she said "transfer student." She leaned in closer and continued. "But I heard he got expelled for pulling the fire alarm before a major test."

A dark-haired boy in a New York Yankees hat and a navy blue blazer pushed his way through the crowd, carrying a ginger ale with a cherry floating on the top and a shrimp kebab.

"Stop, drop, and roll. He's on the move." Alicia handed her silver tray to Dylan and turned to leave. "Don't wait up for me."

"Where are you going?" Dylan squealed. "What am I supposed to do with this?"

"They're name tags," Alicia called over her shoulder. "Get everyone to fill them out before Nina makes her entrance."

Massie watched Alicia follow Josh through the crowd, wishing she had the guts to approach Derrington.

Dylan started filling out the HOLA, MY NAME IS _____ stickers for her friends and stuck them to their clothes. She was about to put one on Claire's pink silk cami when Massie grabbed her wrist.

"Don't," Massie said. "I don't want you to get glue on my new top."

"I had a feeling she was wearing a Massie." Dylan nodded. "No offense, Claire, but I had a hard time imagining you buying a Trina Turk. I actually assumed it was an H&M knockoff."

"Massie said I could borrow it." Claire didn't sound the least bit offended.

Kristen put her hands on her hips and turned to face Massie. "I thought you said anything that needs to be washed in Woolite is OL."

"What's 'OL'?" Claire asked.

"It means *off limits*," Kristen barked. "But I guess you wouldn't know, since it ahb-viously doesn't apply to you."

"And isn't that your handbag?" Dylan pointed at the pink metallic YSL ruffle purse dangling from Claire's wrist.

"Yeah," Massie said to her silver-polished thumbnail. "So?"

"So? So you said you don't lend out anything from this year's YSL line," Dylan snapped.

"Well, it's a new year." Massie looked directly into Dylan's emerald green eyes, making it clear that the conversation was over. She realized this probably wasn't the best time to tell her friends that Claire would be sharing her bedroom. They were acting a little jealous, and she didn't want to rub it in their faces. Besides, they'd have to get used to their friendship . . . eventually.

"Seafood egg rolls?" a waitress asked as she held a tray of fried appetizers in front of the girls.

"How about we trade?" Dylan took the platter and handed the name tags to the waitress. "Please make sure everyone gets one." She turned her back toward the girl and popped an egg roll in her mouth. "Anyone else want?" Dylan asked while she chewed.

"Sure." Claire reached forward and dunked an egg roll in

the plum sauce dish. As she brought it to her mouth, a glob of brown sauce fell on Massie's silk cami.

"Thank Gawd for Woolite." Kristen smirked.

"I am so sorry." Claire's cheeks turned red and her bright blue eyes suddenly looked navy. "I'll save up my allowance and buy you another one. I promise." She grabbed a handful of gold cocktail napkins off the tray and started wiping the brown stain right above her left boob.

"It's okay." Massie's heart was pounding so quickly, she imagined it bursting out of her chest and beating against Claire until she was facedown on the ground begging for mercy. "I'll get some seltzer. . . ."

"Try this." A mysterious hand entered their circle. It was waving a bag of red cinnamon hearts in one hand and a wet white napkin in the other.

"Cam!" A big smile warmed Claire's face.

Massie caught a whiff of the familiar mix of Drakkar Noir and grape Big League Chew that was Cam Fisher. As usual, he was wearing his brother's old leather jacket, but tonight, instead of a tattered white tee underneath, Cam was wearing his Briarwood Tomahawks soccer jersey. He held out a tumbler-sized glass of water for Claire while she dipped the napkin and dabbed the stain.

"Hey," Derrington mumbled, "I heard there was a wet T-shirt contest going on over here." His caramel brown eyes flickered with mischief.

Massie felt her cheeks burn and faced Claire to avoid

Derrington's gaze. But the instant he turned toward his perma-tanned friend Chris Plovert, who for some reason was on crutches, Massie checked him out.

Derrington looked good. His hair was perfectly grown out. Two more weeks and he'd need a trim, but right now his dirty blond strands sat right on top of his dark lashes in a very sloppy-chic sort of way. Unfortunately, he still hadn't gotten over the whole shorts-in-the-winter thing, but his knees didn't look as knobby as they had before the holidays. He must have put on muscle at skate camp. And as far as Massie could tell, they were still the exact same height.

"Well, aren't you going to ask me about skate camp?" he asked Massie.

She twirled the diamond stud in her ear and cocked her head to the side. Massie thought she looked much better at an angle than she did head-on.

"Actually, I was going to ask you why you guys are wearing soccer jerseys to a black-tie-optional party. But if you'd rather start with skate camp, that's fine."

Derrington lowered his head and smiled at his shirt. He looked up at Massie as though he were peering out over the tops of a pair of sunglasses. "It's for good luck. Kind of an old superstition. All we have to do is beat Grayson Academy next week and we're in the finals, which would be so cool, because for the last ten years . . ."

Massie had no idea what Derrington was talking about. Nor did she care. But she nodded her head and squinted, so he'd think she was absolutely riveted. But all she could think about was the puddle of sweat that was forming above her lip. Was it rude to apply a fresh coat of gloss while someone was talking to her? Would he think she was gross if she wiped her mouth with the back of her hand? Was it grosser to let the sweat just sit there? Ugh! Life was so much easier when she was crush-free.

"And we're gonna win." Derrington jumped and turned at the same time, so his butt was facing the inside of their circle. Then he shook it and slapped it a few times. Chris, Cam, Claire, Kristen, and Dylan all cracked up.

Massie rolled her eyes and playfully pushed him out of the circle. "Grow up."

"Oh, please. You love my butt," Derrington teased.

"Yeah, right." Massie instantly hated herself for not coming up with a better comeback. Why did the battery in her brain always seem to die when Derrington was around?

"I hope you'll be there on Friday cheering us on. You can be my good luck charm." Derrington grinned.

Massie instantly tuned back into the conversation. "Of course I'll be there. I *love* soccer."

"Good." Derrington's smile was so sincere, Massie couldn't help smiling too. The twinkle in his light brown eyes made her feel fairly confident that he hadn't met another girl at skate camp. But just to make sure . . .

"Was your skate camp co-ed?" she asked. "Kristen was thinking of going next year, but I told her I thought it was boys only, right, Kristen?"

Massie widened her amber eyes so Kristen would know to play along.

"Uh, right." Kristen adjusted her fedora. It was obvious to Massie she had no idea what she was agreeing to.

"Sorry, it's boys only," Derrington said. "But Kristen, if you wear that hat, they might let you in."

"Very funny." She rolled her eyes. "By the way, you suck as goalie this year. Maybe you should spend a little less time skating and a little more time practicing."

Plovert and Cam laughed at Kristen's jab. Massie joined them, even though she had no idea what goalies had to do in order to "suck."

"What are you laughing at, Plovert?" Derrington shook his head. "You broke your ankle the minute we got there."

"Yeah, and I bet I'm still better in the net than you are."

Everyone laughed except Massie. She hoped they were only joking. It was one thing to be associated with a guy who wore shorts in January if he was a star athlete. But if he really did suck, everyone would think he was a loser. And that would make her an even bigger loser for hanging out with him. Massie closed her eyes and said a quick prayer for the Tomahawks. It was crucial for her reputation that they win Friday's game.

"Please, no one is better than this guy." Todd pushed his way into their circle and put his arm around Derrington.

"Todd, what are you doing?" Claire asked. It was obvious from her tone that she wanted him to leave.

"I thought I'd come and say hi to my new roomie." Todd

released Derrington and winked at Massie. His little friend, Tiny Nathan, covered his mouth with his miniature hand and giggled. "Now that we live together, I feel like it's my duty to keep an eye on you."

"What is he tawking about?" Kristen asked Massie. "Why is he your new roomie?"

"You live together?" Derrington asked. Unfortunately, he didn't sound jealous, just surprised.

Massie wanted to shove the heels of her Jimmy Choo slides up Todd's freckly nose. This was worse than the time she'd caught him eavesdropping on her sleepover. The last thing she wanted to do at this party was fight with her jealous friends about their new living situation.

"Didn't you hear?" Todd asked Kristen. "We're living—"

"Yes, Todd, everyone knows you live in our guesthouse. And in a minute, they are all going to know that you talk to your—"

"Let's go, Nathan." Todd grabbed his friend's skinny wrist and pulled him into the crowd. "I've got a thing for that hottie over by the vegetable platters."

Massie was doing her best to avoid Claire's eyes, knowing she was probably wondering why their living situation had to remain a secret.

"Can I have your attention, please?" Alicia's mother, Nadia, shouted from the top of the staircase. Massie breathed a sigh of relief when Claire turned away to listen to the announcement. Crisis averted.

Nadia was wearing a dark brown strapless paisley dress

and a ridiculously huge necklace made of peacock feathers. Her black hair was wrapped in a tight bun on top of her head and tied with a gold scarf. Even though she hadn't modeled in fifteen years, Nadia looked like she could have walked straight off the runway and into her house. Once again, she asked for attention. Finally, the music stopped and the chatter in the room was reduced to a loud murmur, then silence.

"My husband, Len, and I would like to welcome you all to our home." Her Spanish accent was thick, and Massie had to strain to understand what she was saying. "You know we are always looking for an excuse to get together with friends." A few of the parents started cheering, and Nadia responded with a gracious smile. "And tonight's excuse is a very beautiful one named Nina."

Applause.

Massie searched the room, looking for the guest of honor, but there were no signs of her yet. Nadia was probably trying to build her up because she was such a dork.

"My niece has come all the way from Spain to spend the semester with us. So please raise your glasses and help me welcome Nina Callas to Westchester.

"*Cumplimentar*, Nina!" Nadia toasted.

"*Cumplimentar*, Nina!" the guests toasted back.

A tall, thin girl came out of one of the bedrooms and glided to the top of the stairs. She stood perfectly still, giving the guests a chance to drink her in. She tilted her hips, stuck out her long, thin left leg and let her tanned bare arms dangle by her tiny waist.

There had to be some kind of mistake! This couldn't have been the same busted-up girl Massie had seen in Alicia's vacation photos. Could it? Her black strapless minidress barely covered the label on her underwear. And unfortunately, it looked kind of hot.

"Easy, Gisele," Dylan muttered to no one in particular. "The Victoria's Secret fashion show isn't until November."

Massie laughed louder than she meant to.

"Mee-oww!" Chris Plovert gave a playful smile.

"Yeah, right." Dylan shook her head. "Like I'd ever be jealous of *her*. Her boots aren't even made of real leather."

Nina tilted her long, graceful neck toward the crowd to show off her wide smile and perfectly symmetrical face. A sexy mess of brown wavy hair brushed against her smooth bare back as she turned to show off her perfect profile. She flashed a toothy Julia Roberts smile, then wrapped her elegant fingers around the banister and stepped down onto the marble steps. The bottoms of her high-heeled metallic blue ankle boots sounded like tap shoes as she gracefully made her way toward the main floor. Whistles and whoops filled the air. The people loved her.

Once Nina was finally on the ground floor, she was surrounded by overfriendly admirers doling out handshakes and hugs.

"Gorgeous boots," one of the mothers gushed.

Massie squeezed her eyes shut. She hoped that when she opened them, she'd see the same gawky girl in Alicia's holiday pictures; the one with the unibrow, who wore oversized tie-dyed tank tops and thick white hair bands. But a sultry Spanish beauty with perfect hair had taken her place.

"What's with the hooker boots?" Claire whispered in Massie's ear.

"She's so hyrats." Kristen paused to give her friends a chance to crack her latest jumble. "*Trashy!*"

"Food court!" Massie sneezed.

"I *like* her outfit," Chris Plovert said with a devious smirk.

"Me too." Derrington nodded

Claire glared at Cam.

"Not me." Cam did his best to sound convincing.

Claire smiled.

"Puh-lease." Massie rolled her eyes. "She has no style."

"Her chest makes Alicia's look like a back," Dylan mumbled.

The boys high-fived each other.

"Shhh," Claire shushed. "Here she comes."

Nina glided toward them, never taking her eyes off the boys. Chris Plovert gasped and then punched Derrington in the arm. Derrington giggled and punched Chris back. As Nina got closer, they both punched Cam. By the time she arrived, Nina was faced with three giddy boys and four scowling girls. But before she could say hello, she was pulled away by Alicia's dad, who just *had* to introduce her to Mr. and Mrs. Everhart from down the street.

"Hey, everyone," Alicia announced when she rejoined the group. "This is Josh Hotz. He's new at Briarwood." She was swaying back and forth, twirling the ruby-and-gold ring on her index finger.

"We know Josh," Derrington mumbled. "He's on our soccer team."

"Well, we don't know him." Massie extended her arm. He was the perfect match for Alicia. They looked exactly the same. "Hi, I'm Massie Block."

"Hey, Massie Block." Josh smiled eagerly.

The brim on his New York Yankees hat cast a dark shadow across his chiseled face, but from what Massie could see, he looked like Josh Hartnett, only scrawnier. He was a solid eight. "The chicks in this town are awesome," Josh said after he met Kristen, Dylan, and Claire. His lips were dark red and wet, but not in a gross way. It sort of looked like he was wearing a new line of gloss for men.

"Thanks." Massie pulled on a chunk of her crimped hair. She smiled sweetly and turned to face Josh, hoping her flirty expression would make Derrington jealous. But Josh was staring straight at Nina.

"Uh, let's go meet some other people in my class." Alicia yanked Josh by the sleeve of his blue blazer.

"Will they look like *her*?" he was still looking back at Nina.

Derrington, Cam, and Plovert cracked up. Alicia rolled her eyes and gave his arm one final tug.

"He's a cool guy." Cam was still smiling.

None of the girls responded. Kristen adjusted her fedora, Dylan sucked in her stomach, Claire tucked her overgrown bangs behind her ear, and Massie applied a fresh coat of Krispy Kreme gloss. She cringed when she heard Nina's ah-nnoying *har-har-har* laugh and watched in horror as the tops of her massive boobs jiggled, right there in front of the Everharts.

Massie ran her fingers over the emerald green eyes in her cat brooch, wondering how to keep Nina away from the guys. But when she heard Derrington, Cam, and Chris whispering about "Alicia's cousin's epic cleavage," Massie realized the real problem would be keeping the guys away from Nina.

After the party, Massie rushed home and turned on her G5. It was crucial that her first blog go live before the start of the new semester.

MASSIE BLOCK'S CURRENT STATE OF THE UNION BLOG	
IN	**OUT**
Blogs	Boots (metallic blue only)
Crimped hair	Cleavage
Gift exchanges	Foreign exchanges

"Virgins! Virgins! Virgins!" Massie shouted. Dylan and Kristen joined in. It wasn't long before the entire lunch crowd in the Café was chanting and chewing.

Sage Redwood, a tree-hugging eighth grader, adjusted the garlands in her long wavy hair and straightened the flashing neon VIRGINS sign that hung on the wall above the cash register. It was obvious from her proud smile that she had been waiting for this moment for a long time. She was minutes away from cutting the red ribbon and launching the first alcohol-free cocktail kiosk on campus. And Massie, Alicia, Kristen, and Dylan, who were also known as the Pretty Committee, had received a personal invitation from Sage to be the first girls to try them.

"I can't believe Sage got Principal Burns to agree to this." Dylan shook her head. "These fruity drinks better have a lot of caffeine in them or I'll never make it through World Issues." She was dressed in an all-black pantsuit with pink pinstripes because her mother, Merri-Lee Marvil, the famous talk show host, had told her vertical lines were slimming.

"I miss our Chai lattés already." Kristen tilted the hot pink vinyl rain hat Massie had given her. "Remember when

Sage was handing out those pamphlets last semester about the exploitation of coffee plantation workers in Sri Lanka and marching around the halls waving signs that said, STARBUCKS IS A TOTAL HAS-BEAN?"

"Yeah, didn't I throw iced cappuccino on her?" Massie put her index finger in her mouth and raised her eyebrows innocently as if to say, "Whoopsie."

The three girls laughed at the memory of Sage covered in coffee and fat-free whipped cream.

"Yeah, but she still thinks it was Audrey Capeos." Dylan coughed into her sleeve. Massie noticed that her hack sounded a lot worse than the night before and stepped away from her. She didn't want to be sick and snotty for Derrington's soccer game.

"I love your crimped hair. It looks so rock star." Sage was looking at Massie and twirling a pair of giant silver scissors around her index finger. "I read about it in your blog last night, and I've already asked my mother to get me a crimper next month for my birthday."

"That's so cool, Sage." Massie made a mental note to make crimpers out by the end of the month.

"Speaking of your blog," Kristen piped in, "I love what you wrote about exchange students being out. I mean, what was up with that girl? She seemed so slutty."

"If she's smart, which I doubt, she'll stay far away from me," Massie said. "Because if I ever see her fat boobs near Derrington I'll—"

"Not like Derrington would mind." Kristen's words

crashed down on Massie like a heap of shoe boxes from the back of her closet.

"Hey, Kristen, maybe you should start dressing like her. Then no one would mistake you for a boy," Massie suggested.

Dylan giggled.

"Kahnts a tol."

"You're welcome." Massie was unfazed by Kristen's hurt expression. "Are you ever going to let us see this mysterious haircut?" She reached for the pink rain hat.

"Never." Kristen slapped Massie's hand.

"Ouch!"

Kristen finally smiled.

"Massie, I thought for sure you'd write about your new brooch obsession in your blog." She was looking at Massie's big red rose pin that was fastened to the lapel of her red velvet blazer.

"No way." Massie shook her head. "I want to wear them for at least a week before everyone starts copying me. I'll make them in as soon as I get sick of them."

"Rewtehav," Kristen said.

"Wanna hear something else that's in?" Massie asked. As soon as she said those words, she wished she could take them back. She knew it wasn't the right time, but would it ever be?

"What?" Dylan asked.

Massie took a deep breath. "Bedroom sharing."

"Huh?" Kristen said.

Massie told them that the Lyons family was staying in Westchester and that Claire would be sharing her bedroom until the extreme makeover on the guesthouse was done.

"How long will that take?" Kristen asked.

"Coupla weeks," Massie mumbled.

"Gawd, aren't you two sick of each other yet?" Dylan snapped. "I mean, you just spent the holidays with her in Aspen and now—"

"It may get a little cramped, but it's better than having them move to Chicago, right?"

Kristen and Dylan shrugged and said nothing.

"Hey, speak of the devil." Claire was heading toward the back of the line with her kooky friend Layne. "Over here!" She waved.

Claire was wearing a puffy orange vest, a white sweat-shirt, and navy cotton pants.

Massie heard Dylan whisper to Kristen, "She looks like a crossing guard," but ignored her.

When Claire kept walking, Massie flipped open her cell phone. The bells that hung off her antenna swung back and forth.

"What is your obsession with Claire? Are you dumping us because I have short hair?"

"No, she's dumping us because I'm fat. And we don't have boyfriends like they do."

Massie felt her stomach leap when Dylan said "boyfriends." She couldn't wait to see Derrington on Friday at the soccer game.

"I'm not dumping anyone," Massie snapped. "I just thought Claire could cut the line and wait with us."

"Don't you mean the devil?" Dylan hissed.

"What?"

"You called her that, I didn't." Dylan smirked.

Normally Massie would have fought back, but she was distracted by Nina, who seemed to be modeling the latest knockoffs from Contempo Casuals. Everyone standing on line stopped talking and stared. She swung her butt cheeks slowly from side to side as she passed, hypnotizing the crowd with her steady, confident sway and the click-clacking of her knee-high leopard boots.

She stopped at the front of the line, right in front of Massie.

"*Hola*, I'm Nina." She applied a fresh coat of bloodred lipstick. She snapped the tube shut and reached out her hand. Massie shook it, with caution.

"Funny, I expected you to have a stronger grip." Nina smirked.

"I didn't want your fake nails to snap off."

Kristen and Dylan giggled.

"You are not the first person to think they're fake." Nina held out her nails and admired them. "They're so perfect, no one believes they're real."

"Just like those?" Massie said, looking at Nina's chest.

"Exactly." Nina winked.

Massie couldn't believe the frizzy-haired girl from Alicia's pictures suddenly had so much confidence.

"I love your boots, Nina," Lucy Savo called out as she passed.

"Yeah, they're really awesome," Becky Charsky agreed.

"*Gracias.*" Nina flashed a toothy smile.

Massie casually rolled up the bottoms of her long jeans, revealing the round toes on her new violet Kate Spade pumps, and made a mental note to start wearing shorter pants. Maybe then more people would notice *her* fabulous shoes.

"There you are, Nina. I thought I lost you," Alicia called as she walked toward the Virgins line. She was moving at a normal, casual pace, which for Alicia, a notorious slow walker, meant she was in a hurry. "I'm glad you found everyone."

In a desperate attempt to honor New Year's resolution number seven, which was "Treat all friends with kindness," Massie resisted calling Alicia "Mini-Me." But it wasn't easy, considering that Alicia's hair was styled exactly like Nina's. They were both wearing super-slick, tight ponytails, which Alicia never usually did because she claimed they pulled on her scalp and gave her migraines.

At least Alicia was still dressed like herself. She was in her usual mix of Ralph Lauren separates: Blue Label cargos and a corduroy blazer with a floppy felt flower on the lapel. Nina was wearing super-tight low-waisted jeans that were tucked into her boots and a red faux-fur mini-jacket that barely covered her ribs. Her flat, tanned stomach was completely exposed.

"You better be careful," Kristen said to Nina. "That outfit violates OCD's dress code. You could get suspended."

"Yeah, last time we dressed like that, Principal Burns told us we'd have to start wearing uniforms. If it wasn't for my mother we would all—"

"Puh-*or favor!* I already got sent to that birdie lady's office." Nina sounded proud of her violation. "I told her my outfit was a traditional Spanish ensemble and that taking it off would be an insult to my people."

"And she believed you?" Dylan sounded genuinely impressed.

"I'm still wearing it, aren't I?"

"That is so cool," Kristen gushed. "Massie, I wish you'd thought of that when we got in trouble for wearing our Dirty Devil Halloween costumes to school."

"Uh, I was a little busy trying to plan the first-ever boy–girl Halloween party to think up stupid excuses," Massie said.

"Wait, you just threw your first boy–girl party last October? I've had boys at my parties since the fourth grade."

Dylan sneezed, "Slut."

Massie was the only one who laughed.

"Did you just call Nina a slut?" Alicia snapped.

"Dylan, that's so dure."

"What is dure?" Nina asked.

"It means rude," Kristen offered. "It's jumble."

Nina shrugged.

"No, I swear. That was a real sneeze." Dylan grabbed a napkin off a nearby table. "My cold is getting worse."

Massie wanted to scream. Why were her friends being so nice to Nina? Couldn't they see that she was a manipulative liar? Massie reached inside her hip-hugging Yves St. Laurent money belt and fished around the inside for her latest Glossip Girl flavor. Today's delivery was Cinnabon. It had arrived that morning and it was ah-mazing. It actually smelled and tasted exactly like the warm cinnamon rolls from the mall.

"What is that *aroma*?" Nina asked. She crinkled her button nose and waved her hand in the air.

"Dylan?" Alicia said.

"It wasn't me."

"It smells like my grandmama's kitchen." Nina held her nose. "And she's a terrible cook."

"Yeah, it *is* kinda sweet." Kristen sniffed the air.

Massie turned her back and quickly wiped her lips on the back of her hand.

"Nina, will you be okay here with my friends while I go do my newscast? It's my first one ever, and I don't want to be late."

"Of course, cousin," Nina assured her. "I will be just fine here with your leetle friends."

"Who are you calling leetle?" Massie snapped.

"If the bra fits . . ." Nina half smiled.

Kristen and Dylan giggled. Massie swallowed a big gulp

of air to keep herself from breaking New Year's resolution number seven on the first day of school.

"Don't worry about me, Alicia, I'll be fine. *Buena suerta.*"

"Thanks." Alicia's cell phone rang as she was turning to leave. She checked her Tiffany watch, sighed, then answered. "*Hola?* I mean, hello?"

Massie rolled her eyes.

"Uh, *hola*, Celia." Alicia crinkled her thick dark eyebrows and looked at Nina. "It's your sister," she mouthed.

Nina waved her hand in the air frantically. "Not here," she mouthed back.

"She's calling from Spain." Alicia's expression was urgent.

"I'll call her back," Nina whispered loudly. "When I'm not at school."

Alicia covered the phone with her hand and whispered to her friends, "You should see her sister's wardrobe: it's beyond! They're always in style magazines in Spain and people are always stopping them—"

"Cousin!" Nina snapped. "Just get rid of her."

Alicia relayed the message to Celia and snapped her phone shut.

"Gracias." Relief washed over Nina's face. "I don't have time to give her advice about boys right now. *Dios*, she can be so needy."

Massie nervously twirled her charm bracelet around her thin wrist. How did Nina know so much about boys? Did she ever get nervous when she talked to someone she liked? Would she know how to act around Derrington?

"I'm off to the broadcast booth." Alicia waved. "See you next period."

They watched Alicia weave her way through the clusters of girls gathered around the Virgins kiosk. Once she was out of sight, Massie, Kristen, and Dylan turned and stared at Nina. She stared back at them.

"What?" Nina finally said.

The high-pitched wail of microphone feedback cut through the Café, and everyone covered their ears.

"Sorry," Sage apologized softly into the mic. "It gives me great pleasure to welcome you to OCD's first alcohol-free cocktail kiosk." She cut the red ribbon around the cash register with her giant scissors, and everyone clapped and woo-hooed.

"Welcome to Virgins!" Sage shouted into the microphone.

Nina looked over her shoulder. Gaggles of giddy girls were bumping into her as they jumped and cheered like they were at an Usher concert. She shook her head as if to say, "What a shame."

"Is this place really called Vir-*gins*?" she gasped.

Massie nodded.

"Well, then, I shouldn't be here, that's for sure."

Massie gasped out loud by accident then felt her entire body stiffen out of embarrassment. Now Nina would think she was a prude.

Dylan and Kristen's mouths hung open in shock, but there was also a twinkle of admiration in their eyes, like they were actually impressed.

"Uh, Nina, do you work at 411?" Massie asked.

Kristen and Dylan giggled in anticipation of Massie's next line.

"Huh?" Nina squinted like someone who was having trouble hearing.

"'Cause that was way too much information!"

But deep down inside, Massie was starving for more.

Claire and Layne Abeley were standing at the back of the Virgins line, waiting to place their juice orders. As soon as the cheering died down, Layne turned to Claire and picked up the conversation where they had left off, just before Sage cut the ribbon.

"So why do you think Cam wants to try and kiss you?" Layne stuffed a handful of jalapeño-flavored soy nuts in her mouth, then wiped her salty fingers on her bright yellow Shirley Temple sweatshirt. A green seasoning skid mark was streaked across Shirley's cute little pug nose.

Claire absentmindedly brushed the salt away. "Because he gave me a mixed CD at Alicia's party last night and"— Claire pulled the CD out of her red JanSport backpack— "look at the playlist."

Layne grabbed the CD out of Claire's hand and started reading the names of the songs out loud. "'Do You Love Me,' by Kiss; 'I Want You,' by Kiss; 'I Kissed a Girl,' by Jill Sobule; 'Kiss,' by Prince . . ."

"Shhhhh." Claire knocked Layne in the arm and looked around the Café to make sure no one was listening. "Silent reading, *please*." She watched Layne's narrow green eyes move back and forth across the jewel case while she scanned the rest of the list.

"I've never even heard of these songs," Layne whispered. "Are you sure he didn't steal this from his grandfather?" She was never one to hide her feelings.

Claire rolled her eyes. Why couldn't Layne just be happy for her? "He gets a lot of music from his older brother, Harris," Claire whispered back. "But that's not the point!"

"Sorry." Layne bent down and pulled up her pink socks so that they covered her thick kneecaps. The socks didn't match her yellow ruffled miniskirt and sweatshirt or her orange-and-blue-checked Vans, but that was what made Layne Layne. And Claire had decided a long time ago to accept her for who she was. After all, Layne had accepted Claire back when no one else would, and that was something Claire would never forget. "So *you* want to kiss *him*?" Layne twisted her newly hennaed jet black hair into a messy ball and clipped it with a pink glittery banana clip.

Claire nodded without a moment of hesitation. Then she popped one of Cam's red cinnamon hearts in her mouth and tried her hardest not to chew it. It was a game she had been playing with herself all morning: if she could suck the candy until it disappeared, she and Cam would kiss at the dance. If she bit it, they wouldn't.

"Is that slutty of me?" she asked.

"No, I think it's romantic." Layne gently placed her hand on her heart and made a swooning face.

Claire giggled and turned bright red. "Okay, can we change the subject, please?"

"Sure," Meena said as she and Heather broke into their conversation. "I have a new subject." She pulled a pair of black-and-red-striped leg warmers off her arms and stuffed them in the outside pocket of her Hello Kitty wheelie suitcase. "So, are you really going to be sharing a bedroom with Massie Block?"

"Yeah, are you?" Heather asked.

Their blunt bob haircuts had been dyed the same color as Layne's, and Heather had cut super-short bangs. Claire thought they looked like comic book characters.

Meena and Heather were Layne's best friends and the only other girls at OCD who shared Layne's eccentric style and addiction to protests.

"I think we know her well enough now to stop using her last name." Claire tried to hide her excitement. But it was hard. She loved that people were starting to find out that she and Massie were friends. It did more for her status than the latest Marc Jacobs bag ever could.

"Okay, then is *Massie* really your real friend this time?" Meena pressed. "Or is she just using you again to get something she wants?"

"No, it's real this time." Claire still had a hard time believing it herself.

"Hmmm," Layne said.

"Does this mean you get to borrow her clothes?" Heather adjusted her makeshift belt, which was really a cute stuffed snake that she'd won at Coney Island when she was four. It was so bulky, she was having a hard time keeping it tied around her tiny waist.

"I've already borrowed a ton of her stuff." Claire could feel the proud smile spreading across her face.

"What?" Layne asked.

"Unfortunately, I stained two of her sweaters."

Layne chuckled. "I heard she doesn't have a washing machine—she just throws her dirty clothes out and buys new ones."

"The entire Block estate is built on landfill made up of Massie's dirty clothes." Claire giggled

Layne started laughing, and Claire felt a wave of guilt.

"I'm just kidding. Massie's totally normal."

"Yeah, whatever." Layne rolled her eyes. "You've become a total Massie-chist."

Meena and Heather giggled.

"I have not." Claire felt her throat lock. Why was everyone having such a hard time accepting that she and Massie actually liked each other? Claire searched her mind for a new topic, but she was too flustered to think of anything. Luckily, her cell phone started ringing.

"Hullo?" Claire answered her phone. "Oh, hey—" She was about to say Massie's name but stopped herself. "Really? That's TFFW. We must have walked right past you. . . . We'd love to cut. . . . Be right there . . . ."

"Uh, what's 'TFFW'?"

"'Too funny for words.'"

"Ah," Layne said. "I'm not taking Massie as a Second Language until next semester."

"Very funny." Claire pulled Layne out of the line and led her to the front. "Let's go—Massie said we could cut."

"No, thanks." Meena shook her head. "I'd rather wait back here, with the people."

"Yeah, power to the people." Heather shot her fist in the air.

"Well, we're going." Claire tugged on Layne's arm.

"Someone needs to protect her," Layne shouted to her friends.

"Whatever." Heather chuckled.

"Traitor," Meena yelled with a semi-smile.

Claire was relieved that they had only been teasing. Meena and Heather were so much easier to deal with than Massie's Pretty Committee. They got jealous of each other's CD collections, not each other's friends.

"Hey, no cutting," a few people shouted as they marched past. But Claire kept her eyes fixed forward and ignored them all. She would be with Massie in a few seconds and then they'd be safe.

"Look, Kristen," Nina pointed out when Claire and Layne arrived. "You're not the only one with bad hair. This girl's bangs are way too long."

Claire stuck out her hand. "Hi, I'm Claire."

Nina reached out and shook it hard. "See, Massie, this girl knows how to shake a hand."

Massie put her hands on her hips and opened her mouth to say something, but Claire cut her off.

"Do you really think my bangs are long?"

"*Sí,*" Nina said.

Claire felt everyone's eyes on her. "*Yes!*" she shouted. "I've been trying to grow them out for months."

"I think you should trim them a leetle bit instead. Boys love when they rest just on the tips of your eyelashes. It says, 'Stay by my side. I can't see with all this hair in my eyes and I may need your help crossing the road.' And guys love when girls are helpless."

"*What?*" Massie snapped. "Claire, let me take you to Jakkob after school. He's ah-mazing with layers."

"I would love to," Claire whispered softly. She couldn't help wondering if there was any truth to Nina's theory. "As long as he doesn't scalp me. Cam hates short hair on girls. He says it makes them look—"

Claire felt Massie's thumb poke the side of her ribs and immediately stopped talking. Everyone was glaring at her while Kristen adjusted her pink rain hat. Claire felt a rush of intense heat all over her body, like she had been instantly sunburned.

Nina started laughing.

"Uh, I didn't mean it like that Kristen," Claire said. "I just meant—"

"It's okay." Kristen looked down at the cold concrete floor.

"By the way, Kristen, I love your hat." Layne smiled. "I would totally wear that."

"Great," Kristen said under her breath.

Suddenly, frantic newscast music blasted through the PA system in the Café, rescuing everyone from the awkward conversation.

"What is that?" Dylan screeched.

The music faded out and the *click-clack*ing sound of fingers typing on a keyboard remained.

"It sounds like hail." Kristen covered her ears.

"Good thing you have that hat." Massie rolled her eyes.

Kristen stuck out her tongue.

"I'm kidding!"

Finally, Alicia spoke.

What's up, OCD? I'm Alicia Rivera, kicking off the New Year with a very exciting newscast. . . .

Everyone applauded. Claire could even hear muffled cheers coming from the halls. Alicia must have heard it all the way from the audio booth, because she paused, waiting for the applause to die down.

Claire remembered when Comma Dee used to do the OCD news. She would tell corny jokes and rap the headlines. The entire school would cringe with embarrassment. But the girls in the Café seems to like Alicia's straightforward six-o'clock news delivery, because everyone had turned to face the speakers, anxious for her to continue.

If you've been anywhere near the Café today you know that Virgins is open for business. Congratulations, Sage!

More applause. Sage bowed graciously with her hands in prayer position.

"Easy, Buddha." Massie muttered under her breath.

Today's special juice cocktail is the all-natural fruit-and-soy-based Low-Fat Lover in honor of the upcoming Valentine's Day dance!!!!

The Café exploded with excitement. Napkins were thrown in the air and a few empty fat-free fro yo containers were chucked into the crowd. Alicia quickly changed her tone, as if she could sense the disruption.

Who's ready for the details?

(Cheers)

Alicia giggled to herself like a TV anchorwoman would after bantering with the wannabe-funny weather guy. Claire pictured Alicia sitting at her desk, nervously shuffling her papers, waiting for the right moment to get back to business.

This year's theme is Love Struck. One week from Friday, all the OCD girls will meet at the Briarwood Academy soccer field after the big playoff game to pick dates. But there's a catch . . . literally. The guys will be dressed in Velcro suits, and you will each get five Velcro-tipped arrows. All you have to do is shoot the guy you like and he's all yours. If you don't catch anyone, you have to wait to be asked, unless of course you—giggle!—want to go alone. And as always, the most ah-dorable couple gets the Cupid Award. So I suggest you eat a lot of lean protein Thursday night, wear comfortable shoes, and run like pantyhose. Don't let your dream guy get away. . . .

This has been Alicia Rivera for OCD news saying, I heart you.

(Roaring applause)

"Did you hear *that*?" Massie's amber eyes were wide with excitement.

"Yeah, we have to run!" Dylan whined. "This sucks."

"No, the Cupid Award! If I can get Derrington into a pair of long pants, I bet we actually have a chance of winning."

"Seventh graders never win the Cupid." Kristen shook her head in awe.

"Until now." Massie threw her arms in the air like someone who'd jumped out of a birthday cake to *ta-da* music.

Claire smiled with admiration. She loved Massie's tireless ambition.

"At least *we* don't have to worry about all of that humiliating chasing." Massie turned toward Claire. "It's a total given that Derrington and Cam will stand still for us."

"What makes you so sure?" Nina purred.

"They like us. You know, more than friends," Claire explained. She popped a cinnamon heart into her mouth.

"So?" Nina said. "What if someone else catches them first?"

Claire bit down on the heart. She gasped and covered her mouth with her hand. "Stop being so superstitious," Layne said. "A stupid candy heart can't predict your future."

Claire couldn't believe how well Layne knew her. It was borderline creepy.

"How cute," Dylan huffed. "Not only do you live together but you date together too."

"It's simply ha-darbole." Kristen rolled her eyes.

The girls walked up to the Virgins counter and ordered a round of Low-Fat Lovers. Claire attempted to pay, but Sage simply waved her hand. Claire shrugged, then stuffed her crumpled five-dollar bill back in her pocket. Friendship with Massie Block certainly had its benefits.

"Thanks for the freebies, Sage," Massie said loud enough for the girls on line to hear. She took a long sip of the frothy fruit shake. "Ahhhh. Dee-lish! You know, I would actually consider paying for these. Not that you'd ever want me to, right?"

"Uh, of course not." Sage was always so ah-nnoyingly calm, no matter how hard Massie tried to rile her up.

"Here's to the Love Struck dance and my Cupid Award, of course." Massie raised her juice in the air.

"Cheers," the girls said as they clinked cups. Massie worked her vacant runway-model stare as she led her friends through the crowded Café, flaunting her free drink like a complimentary purse that had just been hand-delivered by Karl Lagerfeld.

Layne leaned over and whispered in Claire's ear, "Hey, how romantic would it be if you had your first kiss with Cam at the Love Struck danoo?"

Claire was overcome by the spicy smell of jalapeño but loved the idea so much, she didn't even flinch. "Brilliant!"

she whispered back. "And you can kiss your boyfriend, Eli, the same night."

Layne made an "ew" face. Claire wondered if she had caught a whiff of her own breath.

"I'm done with him. He wears more makeup than I do, and I'm a little over the morbid skull-and-crossbones jewelry he wears. I think I need to be with someone a little more positive, especially as we get closer to spring."

Nina interrupted. "You know, I am quite an archery expert. I'd be happy to give you lessons. My father taught me how to shoot a bow and arrow when I was a kid. It's the sport of royalty, you know. And Daddy always told me I was going to marry a king."

"Yeah, King Kong," Massie said.

Claire and Layne were the only ones who laughed.

"That would be *meowsea!*"

"I'm sorry, I do not understand this word, *meowsea.*" Nina looked confused.

"Awesome!" Kristen explained. "It would be awesome. The second the guys see my short hair, they're going to run as fast as they can to get away. I need some serious target practice."

"And when they see my fat butt coming, they'll—"

"*You're not fat!*" everyone shouted together.

Dylan pinched an inch of skin on her belly and pointed to it with her free hand. "Tell that to *her.*"

"We need all the help we can get," Kristen confessed.

"Great, then how about Friday after school?" Nina's back was to Massie, Claire, and Layne.

"Uh . . ." Kristen and Dylan hesitated. They must have been thinking about what Massie had done to Alicia when she'd tried to make plans during one of Massie's Friday night sleepovers.

"Uh, is there any other night we could do it?" Dylan asked.

"Yeah," Massie chimed in. "Friday nights I host a very exclusive VIP sleepover party, so that won't work for them."

Claire popped a cinnamon heart in her mouth and tried her hardest not to bite it. But the increasing tension was making it very difficult.

"What's wrong?" Nina flipped her ponytail and leaned closer to Kristen and Dylan. "Can't you make your own decisions?"

Claire bit into the candy and felt the spicy rush of cinnamon burn her tongue.

Massie stuck her hand in Claire's bag of candy and pulled out a handful of hearts. She stuffed them in her mouth and crunched down on all of them at once.

"Since when do you eat candy?" Dylan screeched.

"Since Claire dared me to break into the vending machine at the ski lodge." Massie giggled. Claire started laughing at the memory of on-all-fours Massie jimmying the machine with the pin on her brooch.

"Really?" Dylan looked slightly hurt. "I've been trying to get you to eat sugar for years." She dug her hand into Claire's plastic bag and started gathering a fistful of hearts.

Massie slapped her arm. "Ouch!" Dylan shouted.

"Get your hand out of there," Massie snapped. "You're sick." Then she turned to Nina. "Sorry, Señorita, but you'll have to hang out with people your own age Friday night. My friends have plans."

"Are you sure you don't need lessons?" Nina offered. "It would be pathetic if you didn't shoot anyone and you had to go to the dance alone."

"What about Thursday night?" Dylan sneezed.

"Or tonight?" Kristen asked hopefully.

"Puh-lease." Massie sounded annoyed. "You sound desperate. Any guy at Briarwood would stand still for us." Her cell phone started vibrating. Massie reached into her Granny-Smith-apple-green tote and flipped it open.

"See?" She held the screen in front of Nina's face. "It's a text message from Derrington." She pushed a few buttons and read aloud.

DERRINGTON: Did U hear about the dance?

Massie smirked at Nina and quickly typed her response.
MASSIE: Yup. ☺

Derrington wrote back immediately and Massie read his response to the girls.

DERRINGTON: HOW LAME!

Massie looked confused and continued reading in silence.

Everyone leaned in toward her screen, but Claire was the only one she didn't push away.

DERRINGTON: No way I'm wearing a Velcro suit. 2 stupid! Even Cam thinks it's queer.

Claire felt light-headed and dizzy. This couldn't be happening. What about her first kiss?

"Whatever you do, don't act desperate." Nina sounded smug. "Play hard to get. Make them beg *you*."

"How do you know so much about boys?" Kristen asked.

"Experience." Nina winked.

"Ew," Layne said.

Dylan and Kristen gazed into Nina's dark brown eyes like they were falling in love.

Massie sighed and leaned against the corner of an empty lunch table. She began typing. Everyone stopped walking to wait for her.

"What?" Claire begged. "What are you writing?"

Massie didn't look up from her phone. But she tilted the screen so Claire could see. She seemed to be taking Nina's advice.

MASSIE: No prob. We'll go with other guys. G2G.

Massie hit Send. Claire started chewing on her thumbnail.

"What if that doesn't work?" Claire said under her breath.

"It will," Nina assured her. "My advice always works."

Massie folded her arms across her chest and rolled her eyes. "I wasn't following your advice. I always play H2G."

"Hard to get," Dylan explained to Nina.

Bhuzzzzz, buzzzz.

"It's vibrating!" Claire shouted. "What did he say?"

DERRINGTON: Serious?
MASSIE: 100%. Why?
DERRINGTON: How bout a deal? U & C come watch the playoffs and we'll go 2 the dance w/u.

Claire threw her arms around Massie and started jumping up and down.

"You are so getting your first kiss at a Valentine's Day dance," Layne gushed.

"Be cool," Massie snapped.

Layne covered her mouth.

"He can't hear us." Claire giggled.

MASSIE: Hmmmmm.

"What are you doing?" Claire squealed.

DERRINGTON: Pls. You never come to my games. I need u 4 luck. I want 2 win the MVP ribbon. Deal?

MASSIE: What about Cam?

DERRINGTON: Same.

"Yes!" Claire shouted. "Tell him it's a deal. Tell him!"

"*Wait!*" Nina insisted. "Not so fast or you'll look pathetic."

"OMG, you are sooo good at this." Kristen grinned.

"Yeah, you should do an audio book on how to get guys or something," Dylan gushed.

"Puh-lease. I was totally going to *wait*." Massie reached for another handful of Claire's hearts and checked her watch. "There, I think nine seconds is appropriate."

Nina shook her head and looked away.

MASSIE: Done.

"Looks like we're going to the playoffs," Massie sighed. "Whatever *those* are."

"Meowsea! Now I finally have someone to watch the games with."

"Count me in." Nina smirked. "The only thing I love more than football is the cute players."

Massie leaned in and whispered to Claire and Layne, "If she really loved it, she'd know it was called *soccer*, not football."

They giggled.

"What?" Kristen asked. "Why are you laughing?"

"Is it because I'm fat?" Dylan said.

"*You're not fat!*" Everyone shouted.

"It had nothing to do with you." Massie smirked at Nina.

"Yeah, right." Dylan coughed. She turned her back to Massie.

"I love the way you Europeans call soccer 'football.' It's so ah-dorable."

"I know." Nina slowly turned her head and smirked at Massie. "It is, isn't it?"

"Yeah, if you like sounding clueless," Massie said.

Dylan and Kristen shot Massie a That-wasn't-a-very-nice-thing-to-say look. And Massie responded with a very direct Watch-it-girls-or-I'll-crush-you.

Claire could sense that alliances were starting to shift. She had a feeling that her friendship with Massie would put her on the winning side, but these days, it was getting harder and harder to know for sure.

"Quiet, Bean!" Massie snapped, even though she secretly loved that her puppy was barking at the enormous sweaty man from the Barbarian Moving Co. He deserved it for dropping heavy boxes where ever he felt like it and turning her perfect bedroom into a storage closet.

"This is only temporary," she sighed.

"Huh?" Claire was kneeling on the floor below Massie's bay window, digging though one of the boxes, looking for her pajamas.

"Nothing."

Claire looked up and bit her bottom lip. "Don't hate me because I'm a pack rat."

"As long as you don't hate me because I'm beautiful." Massie tried to mask her frustration, but it wasn't easy. There were six boxes and two scuffed-up army-style duffel bags in the middle of her bedroom. If they had been YSL trunks, maybe Massie could have looked at them without feeling like her eyes were going to bleed. But the only initials Massie saw were *CSL*, for "Claire Stacey Lyons," and they were written in black magic marker.

"Well, that's the last of 'em," said the stocky moving man as he loosened his weight belt and arched his back. He made a loud yawning sound on his way up. "Where are you going to put all of this stuff? This is a big room, but still . . ."

Massie lifted her palm. "My problem." She showed him to the door, slamming it shut when he left.

Claire dropped to her belly and rested her head on a heap of clothes. "He's right. Where are we going to put all of this?"

"Clue: It's green, plastic, and gets picked up every Wednesday morning by a loud truck," Massie said.

"I am so not throwing this stuff in the trash! I've had it since I was little."

Massie clenched her fists so hard, her fingernails dug into her palms. She didn't know how much longer she'd be able to keep up the patient friend routine. She took a deep breath and shook out her hands. "I think it's time for an unpacking montage."

Claire crinkled her blond eyebrows. "A what?"

"You know in the movies? When the characters have to clean up after a raging house party before the parents come home?"

"Oh, I love those scenes." Claire clapped her hands together.

"Well, have you ever noticed how they always manage to get the job done by the end of the song?"

"What song?"

"Whatever song they're playing in the movie."

"Yeah, I guess," Claire said.

Massie pressed Play on her CD player, and "Lose My Breath" by Destiny's Child came blasting through her speakers. "Well, then, get off your butt. Everyone will be here in ten minutes." She started shaking her hips to the beat of the song. "I'm Beyoncé."

Massie lifted Claire's ugly metal tripod and started singing into one of its legs as if it were a microphone.

. . . After I done everything that you asked me
Grabbed you, grind you, liked you, tried you
Moved so fast baby now I can't find you . . .

Claire ran across the room with an armful of sweaters and started dancing with Massie's mannequin. When she thought Massie wasn't looking, she tossed the sweaters under the bed.

"I saw that." Massie laughed. "I'm fine with it if you are." She lifted a pile of Claire's socks and underwear and ditched them on the floor of her closet.

"Fine." Claire shrugged. She lifted the arm of Massie's mannequin and sang into the fingers . . .

. . . Can you keep up?
Baby boy, make me lose my breath
Bring the noise, make me lose my breath . . .

Bean was running from Massie to Claire, back and forth, trying to stay part of the action. When the song ended, Massie hopped over the bags and played it again. She danced across her room, stacking Claire's binders and books on her desk, singing as loud as she could. It was so much more fun pretending to be Beyoncé when someone else was in the room. She didn't feel as freakish as she did when she danced in front of the mirror alone.

Suddenly, the bedroom door burst open. Massie heard herself shriek. But her expression quickly changed to one of agitation when she saw Todd and Tiny Nathan dancing and playing air guitar on Massie's Hermès riding crop.

She marched over to the boys and tore the crop from their sticky hands.

"Where did you get these?" Massie shouted.

"In the back of your closet." Todd yawned casually.

Massie drew back the crop and slapped him twice on the butt, the same way she'd hit her horse, Brownie, when she needed him to giddyap.

"You're dirtier than I thought." Todd gave a devilish grin.

"Get," Massie said as she pushed Todd out of her room, "outta here." She shoved Tiny Nathan and slammed her door behind them.

"Gawd." Massie tossed the crop on her bed. "How ah-nnoying."

"Sorry 'bout that." Claire was obviously embarrassed by her brother.

"It's not your fault." Massie lowered the stereo. She looked around with a satisfied grin on her face. They had stacked all six boxes in the corners and covered them with Massie's colorful silk robes. Nothing had been unpacked, but a walkway had been cleared, which gave the impression that order had been restored.

"Now I'll never find my pjs," Claire whined.

"Here." Massie tossed a pair of burnt-orange satin pajamas at her. "Wear these. They'll look good with your coloring."

Claire smiled and quickly started changing.

"Oh, and wrap this around your waist." She handed Claire a folded brown Dixon. "It will transform those simple satin pajamas into evening wear."

"Uh, okay." Claire slipped her legs through the mesh tube and wiggled it up and around her waist.

Massie stepped into her closet and opened her "delicates" drawer. She sifted through a rainbow of silks and satins until she found her wine-colored boy shorts and the matching baby-doll top. When she was dressed, she climbed up on top of her desk, being careful not to knock over Claire's books, and pulled a gold brooch that looked like the sun out of the cork. She stuck it to one of the straps of her top and jumped down.

"Bean, let go." Claire was sitting on the floor trying to pull one of her striped socks out of Bean's mouth. She finally gave up when she started sneezing uncontrollably and needed both hands to cover her nose.

"Ew, are you catching Dylan's cold?"

"I hope not." Claire was hunched over with her hand covering her face as she made her way into the bathroom.

Massie rolled her eyes when she heard Claire sniffling and blowing her nose.

This is only temporary, she told herself. *Just a couple of weeks.*

"Wanna hear a secret?" Claire called from the bathroom.

"Always," Massie shouted back. She jumped onto her bed stomach-first and propped her chin up with her hands. The heels of her feet took turns hitting her butt cheeks. "How many gossip points is it worth?"

"Zero, 'cause it's about me." Claire stepped out of the bathroom and unhooked her backpack from Massie's doorknob. She stuck her hand inside and moved it around before she continued. Claire looked around the room, then lowered her voice to a whisper. "I am going to kiss Cam at the dance."

Massie bolted up and crossed her legs. "No way! Have you ever—?"

"Nope. It will be my first time." It sounded more like a confession than a statement. "But he's the one, I know it. He was nice to me back when I was wearing Keds."

Massie had no idea what to say. A billion questions went zipping through her head. *How will you know what to do? Are you scared? What if you kiss him and he laughs? What if you're bad at it? What if he tells everyone you're bad at it? . . .*

"Well, it makes perfect sense," Massie assured her calmly. "You two have been together for weeks."

"Yeah, and look what he sent home with Todd today." Claire pulled a plastic bag of yellow, pink, blue, and green hearts out of her backpack. She reached into the bag, pulled out handful of candy and opened her palm. "They have different Valentine's Day sayings on them. At my old school in Orlando we used them for telling fortunes. But these ones are even better, because they are bigger and the messages have been totally updated."

"Huh?" Massie was still thinking about the kiss. *How could Claire be so sure of herself?*

"Ask me a question about boys or love or something." Claire dropped the hearts back in the bag and shook it.

"Hmmmmm." Massie held her big toes and rocked back and forth while she thought. "Okay, will Derrington and I win the Cupid Award?"

Claire made a spooky haunted house sound while she fished around the inside of the bag. She pulled out a green heart and held it in front of her face and squinted to read the tiny letters. **"Love Works in Mysterious Ways."**

Massie jumped off her bed so quickly, she almost landed on Bean. "What is *that* supposed to mean?"

"You have to eat it now." Claire held it out in front of Massie's face. "It's tradition."

"Ew, no, I don't want it." Massie waved the candy away. "I want to try again."

"Why? That was a positive one, I promise. Trust me. I have a lot of experience with these."

Massie took the candy and chewed it as quickly as she could.

"Now you do one."

"Fine." Claire closed her eyes and sat down on the corner of Massie's bed. "Am I going to kiss Cam at the Love Struck dance?" She reached her hand in the bag, grabbed a yellow heart, and read it aloud. **"In Your Dreams."**

Her face turned red and her blue eyes darted back and forth as if she were watching a fly buzz around the room.

"Impossible. You're right; maybe we should try that again."

"Try what again?"

Massie turned toward her bedroom door. Dylan and Alicia had let themselves in.

"Try what again?" Dylan asked a second time. She was wearing white flannel pajamas with pictures of different sushi rolls all over them. Alicia was wearing a gold Japanese kimono with black silk karate-style pants underneath. Her hair was piled high on top of her head in a sexy bun. It was the first time Massie had ever seen it like that.

"Oh, nothing." Massie wished she had worn her black lace nightie instead. "Claire was just saying we should try moving that heavy box again." She pointed to the stack of boxes in the corner. She knew Dylan would have felt left out if she knew what had really been going on. And Massie wasn't in the mood to deal with her irrational insecurities. "Where's Kristen?"

Dylan shrugged. "She said she already had a ride." Then she coughed and took a few seconds to look around. "It's starting to look like my room in here." She coughed some more.

Alicia laughed.

"Relax, it's only temporary," Massie said.

"Where are we going to have our sleepover?" Alicia

asked. "The barn is now a gym, the guesthouse is about to get leveled, and all the other rooms are being used."

"Uh." Massie hadn't even thought about that.

"This is all my fault—I'm so sorry." Claire raced around the room gathering her belongings and hiding them behind Massie's desk and under her rug.

"It's no big deal." Massie was trying to sound convincing. But it was hard. She felt like Claire's stuff was sucking up the oxygen in her room and making it difficult for anyone else to breathe. "We'll just have the sleepover here. It'll be fun." She pressed a small button on the white intercom beside her bed and lowered her face to the speaker. "Inez, could you please bring up five sleeping bags?"

"Yes, of course," Inez's pinched voice answered.

Massie inhaled deeply and tried to relax. She was starting to feel the tension in the back of her neck melt away, until the smell of thick, musky perfume filled her nostrils.

"Ew, what is *that*?" Massie turned toward the odor and locked eyes with Nina.

"*Hola*, Maysee, I was just talking to your father," Nina purred. She was wearing her hair in a sexy bun, just like Alicia. "He is sooo sweet."

Massie's armpits started to sweat.

Nina was dressed in a tiny black slip that had slits on both sides. Tiny crisscrossed laces attempted to hold them together, and Massie couldn't help staring at the diamond-shaped pattern they made across her exposed skin. A pair of metallic gold ankle boots with furry laces completed the look.

"Uh, I thought DVDs weren't allowed at my sleepovers," Massie growled at Alicia.

"They're not." Alicia looked at Dylan and Claire in utter confusion.

"Then why am I watching *Lady and the Tramp*?" Massie glared straight at Alicia, as if Nina weren't standing right beside her.

Dylan busted out laughing and Claire giggled softly into her palm. Alicia widened her brown eyes and gently tilted her head toward her cousin, silently begging for understanding and compassion. She was trying to let Massie know that her mother had made her bring Nina, that she'd had no choice. Of course, Massie picked up on all of this; she spoke that silent language fluently. But she wasn't about to let Alicia off the hook without making her point.

"You know these sleepovers are exclusive. And I never make exceptions." Massie paced around the room, hands clasped behind her back. "But since Nina has absolutely *no* friends her own age, I will let her stay, out of pity. But just this once." Massie turned and looked into Nina's heavily made-up eyes. "Hopefully someone will have found a reason to like you by next Friday night."

"Maybe that someone will be your leetle boyfriend, Derringtons." Nina had a devious smile on her face. "I saw him checking me out during the party last Sunday."

Massie heard her friends gasp and fought the sudden urge to knock Nina right out of her gold boots. Instead, she clenched her fists and sighed. As long as Nina kept calling him Derringtons, with an *s*, she had nothing to worry about . . . . right? But just in case, Massie would make it a point to e-mail him a cute picture of herself from Aspen, just to make sure.

"I've never seen an all-white room before. It's so innocent and virginal. And look." Nina pointed to the mannequins. "Maysee still plays with dolls."

"Those are not dawls. And they probably cost more than your entire—"

"Hey." Kristen was standing in the doorway, her cheeks pink from the cold. She was wearing a black-and-white-plaid flannel nightgown and one of Massie's old rabbit fur hats. "Do you know how hard it is riding a bike in this long thing?"

"Why would you ride a bike? It's winter outside." Nina sounded genuinely concerned.

"I'm trying to get in shape! The girls' soccer playoffs are right around the corner."

Claire nodded her head, like she understood perfectly. But Dylan rolled her eyes and Massie and Alicia giggled.

Kristen looked down at her new black-and-purple Pumas.

"You're very smart. That's probably why you have such sexy, defined legs."

"You think I have sexy legs?" Kristen lifted up the bottom of her nightgown and inspected her calves, as if discovering them for the first time. She looked at Massie, Dylan, and Alicia. "See, I told you I wasn't wasting my time."

"Wasting your time? *Por fah-vor*." Nina sounded horrified. She pointed to Massie's long, skinny legs and chuckled. "Would you rather have weak limo legs, like her?" Nina shook her head in disgust.

"Nina!" Alicia looked at Massie and apologized with her eyes on behalf of her rude cousin.

Massie refused to let her irritation show. Why give Nina the satisfaction? Instead she lifted her palm in a gesture that meant, "No big deal."

I happen to love my limo legs." Massie pointed her toes like a seasoned ballerina. "They're elegant."

"Yeah, if you consider two straws in fuzzy slippers elegant." Nina laughed.

Massie was grateful for the tapping sound on her bedroom door, because she had no comeback for Nina and wasn't about to admit defeat by dishing out a weak "Whatever."

"Come in," Massie called out in her happiest voice.

Inez pushed open the door with the toe on her black rubber clogs. She was carrying a stack of pink and purple sleeping bags that covered her entire face. Massie placed them on the mirrored trunk at the foot of her bed. "Thanks, Inez," she said before closing the door.

"Let's set up." Massie, Claire, Alicia, and Dylan started clearing a space in the middle of the bedroom.

Kristen shuffled across the room in her long nightgown and stood beside Nina. "Do you play soccer, er, I mean football?"

"I'd rather chase the players than the ball," Nina purred.

Dylan and Alicia giggled.

"I like doing both. I'm obsessed with David Beckham," Kristen cooed. "I even set my bike lock combo to his birthday."

"0-5-0-2?" Nina's face lit up.

"Yup." Kristen laughed and high-fived her.

Massie accidentally knocked the stack of sleeping bags onto the floor. "You're starting to look like him, with that haircut." She bent down to pick up the bags, purposely avoiding Kristen's eyes. Massie knew her comment was mean, but Kristen was starting to act a little too BFF-y with Nina, and she deserved a verbal slap.

"You know, Becks's wife, Victoria, had short hair when he fell in love with her," Nina said.

"You're so right." Kristen took off the rabbit fur hat and tossed it on Massie's bed. "I forgot all about that."

Massie laid all of the sleeping bags out in her favorite spoke-'n'-wheel pattern; a perfect circle, with all of their heads facing the center. "Sorry, Nina, I only have five. But I can get you a towel."

"That's okay." Nina dove onto Massie's bed and started bouncing up and down. "I'll just sleep here."

"No, Nina, don't!" Alicia pleaded. "Share my sleeping bag."

"That's okay. The floor is fine for you kids. But I'm thirteen. I *should* have a bed."

"Then go home, grandma! Because this bed is not an option." Massie ran over to Nina and grabbed the heels on her gold boots. "Get *off!*" She pulled as hard as she could, dragging Nina facedown across the duvet. The black slip rode up over her hips and revealed a red thong buried in her butt crack.

Massie shrieked. "Uh, Nina, you've got a letter in your mailbox."

The girls busted out laughing.

Nina started kicking her legs but Massie hung on, her arms flailing around like a spastic Muppet's. She counted to three inside her head and then tugged as hard as she could. "Huu-ahhhh!"

Massie fell back onto the floor with nothing but a pair of tacky gold boots in her hands. "Ew." She whipped them across the room.

"You okay?" Alicia asked Nina softly.

"*Sí.*" Nina turned to Massie. "If you want to try my boots on, just ask."

Massie pretended she hadn't heard that.

"Uh . . . can I try them?" Dylan asked shyly.

"Yeah, me oot?" Kristen jumbled.

Claire managed to keep herself out of the drama by straightening the sleeping bags for the fifth time.

"Of course." Nina smirked. She was looking at Massie.

Massie kicked the boots over to Kristen and Dylan, who descended upon them like a pair of fashion-starved divas. They each grabbed one and slipped it on.

"I brought two suitcases full of boots from Spain." Nina piled her tangled wavy hair back into a bun. "You can borrow them whenever you want."

Kristen and Dylan's eyes lit up. Then they both lost their balance and smashed into each other.

Kristen rested her arm on Dylan's shoulder and pulled off the boot. "They're too big on me," she whined.

"Me too," Dylan sniffled. "What size are you?"

"Six," Nina said.

"Bummer, we're vifes."

Dylan rolled her eyes. "Fives," she explained to Nina.

"Hey, Massie, we should make our own DIY versions of these boots next Friday," Kristen said.

"On!" Massie nodded.

Kristen's face lit up. "Really? Great! I love do-it-yourself crafts."

"Uh, Kris, *on* means *no* in jumble." Massie smirked.

Kristen looked down and pulled an imaginary hair off her flannel nightgown.

An awkward, heavy silence filled the room. No one knew what to say next—not even Massie. She didn't know how much longer she could stand Nina. The girl was like a pair of rayon polyester pants—cheap and irritating.

Purumppppppp

A low farting sound offered a welcome distraction.

"'Scuse me." Dylan waved at the air.

Everyone laughed.

The sound continued and grew louder.

"Sorry. My brother, Todd, plays tuba in the marching band. He's practicing for Friday's game. If he does a good job, the conductor said he can march in the front row during the finals."

Nina covered her ears. "The Lyonses in your country sound more like dying walruses."

Kristen and Dylan laughed.

"He's practicing," Claire insisted. "Give him a break."

"She was kidding," Alicia assured her. "Right, Nina?"

Nina shrugged and stepped into her boots.

"She *was* kidding." Alicia placed a reassuring hand on Claire's back, until she heard her cell phone ring. "Ehmagod, what if it's Josh Hotz!'"

"Why would it be Josh?" Massie asked, wondering why Derrington never called her on the weekends.

"I told him the Laurens were coming over for dinner tonight," Alicia said.

"As in Ralph?" Kristen squealed.

"Yeah." Alicia bit her bottom lip. "Do you think he actually bought it?"

"Answer it!" Dylan prompted

"Hurry," Kristen shouted.

"I'm trying." Alicia strolled leisurely across the room but swung her arms quickly.

Massie darted over to Alicia's navy velvet Ralph hobo bag and pulled out the ringing phone. She tossed it to Alicia, who caught it with one hand, flipped it open with her thumb, and brought it to her ear in one swift motion. She raised her finger in the air, demanding immediate silence.

"Heh-lloooh?" Alicia cooed in a low come-hither voice. Her alert, wide eyes slowly softened . . . and then shut. "Oh, *hola*, Celia." Alicia sounded tired and bored. "It's for you," she mouthed to Nina.

Nina waved her hand. *"Mañana,"* she whispered back.

"Celia, she'll call you back tomorrow." Alicia snapped her phone shut. "Why won't you talk to your sister?" she asked Nina.

"She's boring."

"Can we please do something fun?" Massie insisted.

"Like what?" Dylan asked.

"Let's play Wear or Dare," Massie suggested.

"Yeah!" everyone shouted.

"Is that some sort of little kiddie game?" Nina asked.

"No, it's fun," Claire promised. "If you don't do the dare you have to wear—"

Nina interrupted. "Who wants a sexy Spanish makeover?"

Kristen and Dylan's hands shot straight up in the air, but Alicia only lifted her arm halfway.

"You should start with a brush and some makeup remover," Massie mumbled.

Claire covered her mouth and giggled.

Alicia lowered her arm.

Nina walked over to the sleeping bags and sat down on Massie's. She dumped a bag full of exotic Spanish cosmetics on the floor and swished them around like a card dealer trying to mix up the deck.

Massie pointed her speakers directly at Nina, then

blasted her Destiny's Child CD. She laughed to herself as she hurried into her bathroom to grab her hair crimper. "Who wants to get crimped?"

"Very funny." Kristen tugged on her short blond hair.

Nina touched Kristen lightly on the arm and mouthed, "Let it go."

Dylan tossed her thick curly red hair over her shoulders. "If you crimped my hair, I'd never be able to squeeze myself out the front door."

"You look absolutely beautiful just the way you are, Deelan."

Dylan smiled and slid closer to Nina.

"You can do mine," Claire offered

"And mine," Alicia agreed.

"Done."

Massie plugged the crimper into the socket, piled a stack of decorative purple goose-down pillows against her headboard, and leaned back.

"Come, sit." She patted her duvet.

Alicia and Claire sat in front of her with their legs crossed.

The red light flashed on the side of the crimper. "It's ready." Massie reached for a chunk of Claire's white-blond hair and pressed it between the hot corrugated plates. When she released it, a waft of smoke drifted toward the ceiling, and Claire's hair was crinkled.

Claire felt the back of her head. "This feels so cool. I want one."

"It looks ah-mazing." Massie reached for Alicia's hair next.

"So, Deelan, who are you going to ask to dance?" Nina was shouting above the music and pressing a glittery fake eyelash on Dylan's small eyelid. Kristen was beside them, lining her lips with a burgundy pencil.

Massie was eavesdropping on their conversation while she crimped Alicia's hair. The more Nina said to her friends, the harder Massie gripped the iron.

"Do you smell something burning?" Alicia asked.

Massie quickly released her grip and waved the gray cloud of smoke away from Alicia's singed hair. "No."

"I dunno who to ask yet." Kristen bit her lip.

"Me either," Dylan murmured as Nina pressed the lash against her eye.

"Just pick the best kisser." Nina nodded.

"Who's that?" Kristen asked.

"You don't know?" Nina dropped the lash on Dylan's sushi pajama top. "*Dios*, you act like you've never made out with anyone before."

Kristen was silent. Dylan sneezed.

Nina looked up at the bed. "Of course you've all kissed boys before, right?" She stood up. "*Right?*"

Massie's heart started to race. She couldn't let Nina know the truth. "I don't kiss and tell." She silently prayed that Claire and Alicia would back her up. And they did, by keeping their mouths shut.

Nina walked over to the round dimmer switch on

Massie's wall and turned down the lights. Then she sauntered over to Kristen and Dylan while twirling one of the
dangling laces from her slip around her finger. "How about
we make this interesting?" she said. "I will give three pairs
of my boots to the first girl who kisses a boy at the dance."

"But they're too big," Dylan complained.

"EBay," Kristen whispered.

"Or thick socks. This goes for you too." Nina turned
toward Massie, Alicia, and Claire.

"I wouldn't even burn those hooker boots for warmth."
Massie pressed down on a chunk of Claire's hair with the
iron.

"Claire?" Nina offered

"Nah. I want my first kiss with Cam to be romantic, not
part of a bet."

Claire had no problem admitting she was a lip virgin,
and Massie secretly wished she had the luxury of being that
honest. But a statement like that would probably ruin her
reputation.

"Cousin?" Nina asked Alicia.

Alicia looked at Massie, then at Nina, then at Massie
again. "Uh, that's okay. I'm good."

Nina stood over Kristen and Dylan. "I guess it's just you
two."

"I'm in." Kristen giggled. "I'll go for Kemp Hurley. He's a
total perv. I heard he holds his cell phone under girls' skirts
and takes pictures of their underwear. He'll totally want to
make out."

Massie was shocked. When had Kristen become so slutty?

"I'm in too." Dylan coughed. "I'll go for Chris Plovert. The whole leg cast thing will make it easy for me to catch him. I won't have to run at all."

"Who are you going to go for?" Alicia asked Nina.

"I'm going to leave it open."

"That's social suicide." Alicia's eyes were wide. "There won't be anyone left."

Nina turned to face Alicia. "*Por fah-vor*, look at me. I can get anyone I want."

"Puh-lease." Massie slammed her crimper down on her night table. She marched over to the dimmer switch and turned the lights up to maximum brightness. "Look at your style! You are a walking *don't*!"

Claire cracked up. Alicia semi-smiled, then bit her lip.

"You girls better be nice to me." Nina pretended to string three arrows in a bow. "Or I just might go after Derringtons, Cam, and Josh. There's no rule that says I can't shoot all three."

Massie felt a sudden wave of nausea. She didn't have to be an archery expert to know that Nina had perfect form. And she would hardly be afraid to use it.

"And what makes you think they'll actually want to go with you?" Massie countered.

"These." Nina pointed to her gigantic boobs.

Massie's insides froze. She had finally met her match.

Massie and the girls woke up to the sound of a wrecking ball smashing into the guesthouse.

"It sounds like your bowling birthday party," Dylan said to Kristen.

"Only a billion times louder," Kristen agreed.

They shimmied out of their sleeping bags and threw open Massie's curtains. In a mater of seconds, the stately stone cottage was reduced to a pathetic heap of rubble and rocks.

"Cooool," they all whispered before returning to the warmth of their sleeping bags.

The backyard was flooded with the milky gray light of January. Usually the bare shivering trees outside her window made Massie feel cold, lonely, and sad, even if nothing was bothering her. But this morning she felt fine. She wasn't even dreading the moment when her friends' parents would pick them up and take them home, because for the first time Massie wouldn't be left alone. Claire was there.

When the doorbell rang, all the girls jumped up and started gathering their stuff. But Claire sat peacefully on her sleeping bag, painting her toenails metallic blue. Even though her curved spine made her look like a harp and half of her hair was crimped while the other half was super-straight, Massie was overcome with appreciation for her roommate.

There was a light knock on the door before it opened. "Girls, Alicia's driver is here." Kendra was dressed in a tight black unitard and had tied an emerald green Hermès scarf around her tiny waist. White stretch socks swallowed her tiny calves and vanished into a pair of metallic red Nikes. A red-and-white-striped visor that said MEOW in red rhinestones kept her freshly highlighted hair away from her face.

"Mom, you look like the Cat in the Hat." Massie wished her friends didn't have to witness such a brutal outfit.

Claire looked up. Her eyes were red and puffy and the tip of her nose looked purple.

"What's wrong with my Versace exercise suit?" Kendra turned around as if she were chasing her own tail.

"I think its super-cool," Nina promised.

"Of course *you* do," Massie hissed.

"It looks so good on you, Mrs. Block." Nina oozed charm. "How do you stay so fit?"

"Nina, you are so sweet." Kendra blushed. Her smile was wide and sincere, despite her recent injection of Botox. "We converted our horse shed into a gym, so I've been working out a lot lately. I have a trainer coming over in ten minutes to teach a Pilates-cardio-kickboxing-Ashtanga-yoga class. You can join us if you like."

Massie shot Alicia a desperate glance.

"Uh, thanks, Mrs. Block, but Nina—"

Alicia was cut off.

"I would love to." Nina clapped her hands together. Then her expression changed to one of regret. "But I don't have any workout clothes here."

"Oh, that's no big deal." Kendra bounced over to Massie's closet and tugged on her feather boa to turn on the light. "Borrow anything you'd like."

Massie couldn't stand it when her mother treated strangers like family.

"That would be great. Thanks, Mrs. B." Nina stood up and walked over to the closet.

"Oh, please sit down," Massie offered in her sweetest voice. "Let me get something for you."

Massie stepped into her closet and pulled out an old sweat-stained wife-beater and a pair of tight Adidas sweats. They were blue with white stripes running up the sides. She quietly reached for a Prada shoe box off one of her shelves and pulled out a pair of squeaky scissors and quickly cut a hole in the butt.

"Here you go." Massie held out the clothes for Nina. "Sorry I can't give you any sneakers—I'm a size five and you're a six."

"That's okay, I'll wear my boots. It's good for my calves." Nina stepped out of her black slip in front of everyone and slid on the pants.

Dylan, Kristen, and Alicia saw Nina's butt cheek sticking out and started laughing. Massie lifted her index finger to her mouth and slowly shook her head.

Kendra didn't notice. She was crouched down beside Claire, examining her face.

"Claire, we have to get you to a doctor." Kendra sounded alarmed. "Your face is all puffy and red. You're having a reaction. Do you have any allergies?"

Claire hesitated and avoided Massie's eyes. "Uh, sometimes I can be allergic to dogs but—"

"Bean!" Kendra said.

The dog shot out from under Massie's bed like a hairy bullet and ran out of the room.

"I'm sure I'm just catching Dylan's cold," Claire promised.

"Uh, no offense, Claire, but I don't look like a Sharpe. You have something else."

Massie elbowed her in the ribs. "It's not Bean. That's impossible."

"Is my mom here?" Claire asked Kendra.

"She went to some crafts fair down at the church. Why? Are you having trouble breathing? Is your throat locked? Can you swallow?"

"I'm okay," Claire whispered softly. "Just a little hot and itchy."

"Then we'll deal with this after my class. Ready, Nina?"

"*Sí.*" Nina doused her neck in musky perfume and skipped out of the room behind Kendra.

Massie could feel the weight of her hanging jaw.

"Sorry." Alicia threw her red Coach weekend bag over her shoulder and shrugged. "I won't bring her again. I promise."

You better not, Massie wanted to say, but she couldn't speak. She felt like someone had filled her entire body with gooey Marshmallow Fluff. It was hard enough to watch Nina and her mother bonding, but Claire's Bean allergy? Massie couldn't believe her luck. Now Claire would have to leave.

Massie paced around her room, tidying. She placed three crystal bowls filled with pretzel crumbs and melted Junior Mints outside her bedroom door so Inez could take them to the kitchen. While she straightened her bed, Massie tried to think of something positive about Claire leaving to keep herself from crying. At least her room would be tidy again. And that was positive, right?

Claire was rolling up the sleeping bags, sniffling, probably thinking about the same thing. But Massie had no comforting words. If she had, she would have used them on herself.

"Where's my hair crimper?" Massie checked the night table, looked between her sheets, felt under her bed, and lifted up her pillows. It was gone.

"I dunno," Claire mumbled from behind the stack of pillows she was holding in her arms.

Inez tapped lightly on the door and then let herself in. She was carrying a wicker laundry basket filled with fresh linens. Like a robot programmed for efficiency, Inez dropped the basket on the floor and walked straight over to Massie's bed. She tore the sheets off, rolled them into a tight ball, and stuffed them in the basket. In a matter of minutes the bed was dressed in a brand-new set of white sheets and pillowcases.

"I like my purple sheets. What are you doing?"

Inez bent down and lifted up the tiny puppy. She dropped her in the laundry basket and tucked Bean's bed under her free arm.

"I have to get rid of all things that are covered in dog," Inez announced.

"What? *Why?*" Massie screeched. She could hear Bean whimpering inside the basket.

"Mrs. Block said so." Inez swiftly made her way to the door. "To fight the allergies."

"Nooooo!" Massie shouted. "She can't do that!"

Bean started barking.

"You think I like it?" Inez scowled. "Mrs. Block says now the puppy dog sleeps with me!" She slammed the door shut behind her.

Massie turned and looked at Claire's puffy face. "How could you just stand there and let that happen? Why didn't you tell them that it was just a cold?"

Claire scratched a welt that had formed on the side of her neck. "Because it's not. But give me a chance to fix—"

"How can you fix this? They took my dog away!" Massie felt dizzy and leaned against the side of her desk. "How would you like it if someone came into your house and just took Todd away?"

"You can't compare your dog to my brother." Claire was rolling the bottle of blue nail polish between her palms.

"I just did!" Massie shouted.

Right on cue, Todd started blasting his tuba, *off key!*

Massie pounded on the wall. "I wish someone *would* take him! Then you could have his room and I could get Bean back."

His tuba suddenly got louder, as if he had moved closer to the wall on purpose.

"Your family is destroying my life!"

Claire's blue eyes seemed to harden and turn a shade darker. She was obviously offended, but Massie was too upset about Bean to apologize.

"I'm destroying *your* life?" Claire's body shook with anger, which must have loosened the tears behind her eyes and sent them spilling down her cheeks. "How can you say—?" She was rolling the nail polish bottle faster now, and the top accidentally came off in her hands. Metallic blue splattered across the burnt-orange pajamas Massie had lent her.

Claire looked up at Massie, her eyes wide and her mouth open, like someone had jumped out from behind the bed and soaked her with a water balloon

"How can I say that? How can I say that?" Massie asked. "You ruin everything of mine!" She marched into her bathroom and slammed the door shut. Before she burst out crying, Massie turned on the two swan-shaped faucets over her sink, then blasted the water in the shower. No one was allowed to hear her cry except Bean. And *she* was gone.

After ten minutes of sobbing, Massie's anger had subsided and a weak, feverish feeling had taken its place. She was ready to negotiate with Claire. Perhaps they could come to some sort of Bean compromise. Maybe Claire could sleep under a mosquito net or wear a surgeon's mask? And she could always get another pair of burnt-orange pajamas, right? Massie shut off the water and turned the shiny silver handle on her bathroom door. She stepped into her bedroom cautiously, not exactly sure what she was afraid of.

"Claire?" Massie asked meekly. "You in here?"

"Yup." Claire's voice sounded muffled, like she was inside a box.

"So am I," another muffled voice chimed in.

Massie poked her head inside the closet and saw Claire standing with Layne.

"What are you doing here?"

"I told Claire I'd come over today and help her unpack." Layne was wearing a pink rain hat similar to the one Kristen had been wearing at school the other day and a hot pink jumpsuit that was unzipped just enough to show a sliver of the black-and-yellow-striped sweater she was wearing underneath. She had a beige canvas backpack strapped to her shoulders.

"What are you wearing?" Massie asked. "Did you sky-dive here?"

"You know, you didn't really give her much closet space to work with," Layne said.

"It's okay, Layne." Claire pushed Layne out of the closet.

"No, it's not, it's totally unfair," Layne insisted.

"Hey, Layne, knock knock." Massie put her hands on her hips.

Claire sighed.

"Who's there?" Layne asked, happy to help.

"Butt out."

"Butt out who?"

"Butt out, Layne!" Massie turned on her heel and marched out of the closet. She slammed the door behind her and locked it, leaving Claire and Layne trapped inside. It was the first time she giggled all day.

"Let us out." Layne pounded on the door. "Or I'll wipe jalapeño salt all over your precious cashmere sweaters."

"Go ahead. Claire has already destroyed half of my wardrobe. You might as well finish the job. See you later," Massie shouted. "Good luck with your reorganizing." She stomped on her wood floors, pretending to leave. After a few seconds, Massie quietly removed her diamond studs and pressed her ear against the door.

Layne was panting.

"She'll let us out eventually. Don't panic. So what's up?" Claire was obviously trying to take Layne's mind off the fact that they were trapped. "How's Eli? Are you two still hot and heavy?"

"I dumped him last night on IM. I wrote, 'U G2G 4Ever.'"

They giggled.

"Why?"

"He told me he bumped into Alicia and Nina at the MAC makeup counter," Layne said.

"So you finally got tired of dating a guy who wears eyeliner?"

"No, he became obsessed with Nina. He wouldn't stop talking about her. He loved her sexy boots, her wild outfits, and her exotic accent. I swear, Nina-mania is spreading faster than Dylan's flu."

"Let's ask the hearts about her."

"'Kay," Layne agreed. "Hearts, should we lock up our crushes? Is Nina a boy-snatcher?"

Claire giggled. Massie pressed her head against the door a little harder. She heard the plastic bag rustle and the candy hearts clink together.

"It says, '*She*-devil.'"

Massie felt her stomach sink when she heard Claire and Layne gasp. She wanted to run in the closet and ask them to help her come up with a plan to get rid of Nina.

"That girl must be stopped," Layne shouted. "It is our duty to put an end to Nina the Sex Machina."

Just then, Massie's cell phone rang. She fumbled to hit ignore, but it was too late.

"Massie, are you out there?" Claire shouted.

"Open the door." Layne pounded.

"Come on, Massie, we have a movie to catch," Claire pleaded.

Massie unlocked the door with one hand and answered her phone with the other.

Layne and Claire burst out of the closet and stormed out of the bedroom.

Massie ignored them.

"Hullo? . . . Hey, Kristen, what's up? . . . Your bike lock

is missing? What about your bike? . . . Who would take the lock and leave the bike? . . . Well, I can't find my crimper. . . ." Massie searched her room to see if anything else was gone. That was when she noticed an empty space on her Glossip Girl shelf where her tube of Cotton Candy had been. "I think I know who did this." She thought of the ten minutes she had spent in the bathroom while Claire was alone in her room. She could have called Layne and told her to swipe the lock on her way into the house. Massie had seen Little Miss Innocent do some pretty sneaky things when she was upset and knew that stealing was hardly beneath her.

"I'll look into it. I have a few ideas. I'll call you back in a bit."

"'Kay," Kristen said before she hung up.

Massie crept down to Inez's room and dog-napped Bean. She raced upstairs and let the dog roll around and play in a pile of Claire's clothes.

"Payback's a bitch." She patted Bean on the head. "Pun intended."

MASSIE BLOCK'S CURRENT STATE OF THE UNION BLOG	
IN	**OUT**
Dance contests	Kissing contests
Colds	Allergies
Soul mates	Roommates

Claire was sitting in the backseat of the Blocks' Range Rover with her forehead pressed against the cold window. It was all she could do to keep herself from barfing.

"Todd, could you stop playing that thing for one second?" Claire shouted toward the very backseat.

"I have to practice," he said into his tuba. "I'm playing at halftime today."

"Well, it's making me nauseous."

Todd lifted his swollen lips away from the mouthpiece. "I'm not the one driving."

"Todd!" Judi shouted over her shoulder.

He responded with a short toot.

"Mom, ease up on the brakes a little," Massie snapped after her head jerked forward.

Claire was relieved someone had finally spoken up about Kendra's horrible driving.

"It's not me, it's my shoes," Kendra promised. The car jerked three more times as she made the turn into the parking lot at Briarwood Academy. "These new Prada wedge heels have a bit of weight to them."

Claire's mother, Judi, laughed and sighed. "Oh, Kendra, you and your shoes. You are so funny!" But Claire knew her mother didn't really see the humor in a grown woman who blamed her spastic driving on designer footwear. But lately everyone had been trying to act more tolerant of one another. "There's a spot," Judi shouted.

Kendra slammed on the brakes and Claire's head knocked against the window. Massie chuckled, then reached into her midnight blue feather clutch and pulled out what must have been her most recent Glossip Girl delivery, because Claire didn't recognize the spicy scent. She watched though the corner of her eye as Massie smeared the stinky gloss across her lips. For the past week, Claire has been very careful not to show any interest in anything Massie did. Not until she apologized for accusing Claire of destroying her life. In fact, she was only riding with Massie because they'd promised Cam and Derrington they'd go to the game if the boys would stand still during the Love Struck dash. And Claire had every intention of honoring her deal with Cam, even if it meant sitting with Massie, driving with Kendra, and listening to Todd's tuba.

"Ew, this smells like butt!" Massie pulled a road atlas out of the seat-back pocket and wiped her lips on Ohio. "I knew Taco Belle would be gross!"

Claire's body shook as she tried to suppress her laughter.

"Why didn't you steal this one instead?" Massie hissed.

Claire was tired of denying Massie's accusations. She had been doing it all week. It was time to try a different approach.

"I don't like Mexican food. But if you get mac 'n cheese, I'll take it."

"Just like you took my cotton candy?"

"Exactly." Claire turned to the window.

Kendra stepped on the brake and looked at Massie through the rearview mirror. "Why are you two so dressed up for a silly soccer game? We're only here to see Todd play his flute in the marching band."

"Tuba," Judi corrected. "Todd plays the tuba."

Massie looked down at her blue tights, black leather miniskirt, and her matching knee-high boots as if she were noticing her outfit for the first time. "I would hardly call this 'dressed up.'" She made air quotes around *dressed up*. "These boots are almost three months old."

"Well, Claire is certainly looking a little more formal than usual." Judi turned around and examined her daughter. "What's the occasion?"

For the first time in seven days, Claire looked Massie in the eye. She was silently begging her not to tell the mothers that they were really dressed up for Cam and Derrington. Claire knew her mother would want to take pictures of her chasing Cam with a bow and arrow after the game. And she had already been humiliated enough over the last few months.

"Since when did it become a sin to wear my green lace Christmas dress to a soccer game? What's the point of buying something if you're only going to wear it once a year?"

"Oh, I can think of a million reasons." Kendra smiled and slapped Judi playfully on the arm.

"Besides, I'm wearing it over jeans, which gives it a casual look," Claire shouted over Todd's tuba.

Massie reached behind her and pinched Todd's thigh until he stopped playing. "If by *casual* you mean *homeless*, then yes, it does." After she finished speaking she let go.

"Outfits aside, I think it's nice that you're all here to support Todd." Judi sounded pleased. Claire couldn't help looking at Massie after her mother said that. And to her surprise, Massie looked back at her with a wink and friendly half-smile. Claire smiled back.

"I know he appreciates it. Don't you sweetie?" This time Judi twisted her neck so she could see her son's grateful expression.

Todd blew two long, moaning blasts that sounded like a foghorn. Claire and Massie turned around and slapped his legs at the same time, then giggled.

Kendra finally parked the car and everyone jumped out. Claire was tempted to kiss the ground but took five deep breaths instead and asked her mother for ginger ale money. Judi handed her three dollars and made the girls promise to meet back at the car after the game.

"Uh, we have this thing for school after the game," Claire called back over her shoulder. She looked to Massie for help. The last thing she wanted was her mother watching her run around a soccer field chasing boys on a Friday night. Luckily, Massie felt the same way.

"Yeah," she shouted. "Dean, Alicia's driver, will take us home. We'll be back before dinner. Good luck, Todd!"

"Thanks," he said into his tuba.

"Have fun," the moms called as they waved goodbye to their daughters.

Massie led Claire straight to Kristen, who was sitting in the first row of bleachers behind the home bench. She was dressed in head-to-toe orange-and-blue Briarwood Tomahawks gear, waving a pennant in the air, and jumping up and down.

"I can't wait to see what you do when the players actually get on the field." Massie smirked.

Kristen laughed. "Hey, I love that you're here," she said. "I hate coming to these things alone.

"You'd never know it." Claire craned her neck, looking for a soda cart.

A father with a beer belly in a black leather jacket smacked Kristen on the back. "Hey, good luck today, buddy." He turned sideways and stepped into the opposite row of bleachers.

Kristen crinkled up her blue eyes, stuck her tongue out at the man, and shouted, "Ttub leoh!"

Claire and Massie covered their mouths with their gloved hands and laughed.

Kristen reached into the pocket of her Tomahawks windbreaker and pulled out a tube of red lipstick.

"When did you start wearing *that*?" Massie asked.

"When people started thinking I was on the boys' soccer team," Kristen snapped.

The girls giggled as she overdosed on Revlon's Paint the Town Red.

Once the game finally started, Kristen seemed to forget her anger. She screamed for the Tomahawks every time they had the ball, while Claire mostly just shouted for Cam. She hit Massie every time Derrington made a good save so she'd know to cheer for him. But aside from those Derrington moments, Claire and Kristen were on their feet rooting, while Massie sat bundled up in her sheepskin coat and two scarves, playing Breakout on her cell phone.

"Virgins!" A voice shouted. "Get your virgins here."

Sage Redwood was balancing a tray of her signature juice drinks while another girl walked beside her collecting money.

"I'll take one." Claire waved, giving up on her ginger ale.

"Do you have any Perrier?" Massie looked at Kristen and then said, "Make that two."

Ever since Massie had found out Kristen was poor, she bought everything for her—lunches, movie tickets, snacks, accessories, and glittery school supplies.

"How about one of our Virgins for Life T-shirts?" Sage's helper opened her jacket and showed Massie that she was actually wearing one herself. The edges of Massie's mouth start to curl up and Claire knew that a clever cut-down was on its way out.

"I'd buy one, but I can't stand false advertising," a voice announced. It wasn't Massie's.

Nina and Alicia were behind Sage, waiting to squeeze

past her and sit down. They were both wearing their hair in Pocahontas braids. But the similarities stopped there. Alicia was dressed like she always was, crisp dark jeans, a cute cami, a Ralph Lauren blazer, and her long gray coat, while Nina was wearing a J.Lo version of a soccer uniform: denim short shorts and thigh-high platform sneaker boots. A thin white long-sleeved T-shirt with the number 69 written on the back in rhinestones completed the outfit. Throughout the game guys kept offering her their coats, but she swore that she was a hot-blooded animal and didn't need them. Then she would growl.

"Oh, by the way." Nina turned to Massie. "Thanks for the air-conditioned exercise pants. Being exposed like that gave me such a thrill."

"I'm sorry, I'm having a hard time understanding what you're saying," Massie snapped. "I don't speak Slut."

Nina ignored Massie and turned to Kristen. "You look so pretty today. I love the lipstick."

"Really?" Kristen beamed. "Thanks so much." She reapplied her lipstick and turned to Nina. "I'm glad you're here."

Claire felt like she was going to puke all over again. Nina was more nauseating than Kendra's driving. She turned and focused on Cam, who had just taken the ball away from one of the Grayson guys. "Yeah, Cam!" she shouted. But just as quickly, the ball was taken from him. Number 37 kicked it across the field and passed it to number 20, who kicked it toward the net. Derrington stuck out his arm and managed to block the goal. Then he turned to the crowd, pulled down his shorts, and wiggled his bare butt.

Everyone jumped out of their seats and cheered for the star goalie.

"Massie!" Claire shouted. "Get up—Derrington just made a great save."

Massie stood up on her bench and started bouncing up and down. Cam and Derrington waved at them from the field and Claire felt her heart leap. Massie looked over at Claire and smiled with her eyes.

"You're welcome," Claire said.

"The better he plays, the easier it will be for us to win the Cupid Award." Massie turned to Claire. "Don't you think?"

"Let's see." Claire pulled the bag of candy hearts out of her coat pocket. "Hearts, will Derrington win the Cupid Award?"

"Let me do it." Massie stuck her hand in the bag and pulled out a blue heart. **"Destiny."** Her face lit up and she smiled brightly. "Yes!" She popped the candy in her mouth and hugged Claire. "I love these things. Why didn't I think of doing this?"

Claire figured that was Massie's way of apologizing and decided to accept.

"Isn't this stupid game over yet?" a dark figure asked as she pushed her way in between Claire and Massie. She was wearing a black poncho, black sunglasses, and a black pashmina wrapped around her flaming red hair.

Massie leaned over and lifted the sunglasses off the mysterious stranger's face. "Dylan?"

"Shhhh. If my buther knows I came here, she'll kill be. She thinks I'm doo sick do be out in the cold, but there's doh way I'b gonna let someone else shoot Chris Plovert." She broke into a coughing fit.

"Wait, you don't have a brother," Kristen piped in.

"Buther, not brother. *Buther!*"

"Is that a jumble?" A hopeful smile spread across Kristen's face.

"I think she's trying to say 'mother,'" Claire offered.

"I ham," Dylan sighed. "I'm just doh duffed dup."

"Dylan, did you lose weight?" Nina asked. "You look so slim."

"Really?" Dylan smiled. "Maybe it's because I'b wearing black."

"I think it's because you have a very sexy figure." Nina smiled.

"Thanks, Deena. You look really good in those shorts."

Claire looked at Massie and stuck her finger down her throat. Massie giggled.

"Is dis another inside joke between you two?" Dylan barked.

"*No!*" Claire and Massie shouted at the same time.

"Whatever." Dylan rolled her eyes. "Does anyone have any gloss? By lips are chapped."

"Here, you can keep this." Massie gave Dylan her tube of Taco Belle.

Dylan spread the wand across her lips. "Ew!" She whipped the tube onto the soccer field. "Even I can smell dat! Dince when is Sweaty Butt a lip gloss flavor?"

Everyone burst out laughing.

"Here, try mine." Nina passed a gold tube of gloss down the row. Then she blew a huge pink bubble with her gum and smiled when it popped all over her shiny lips.

Dylan sniffed it and smiled. "Better. I don't dmell a thing. Dhanks."

"Lemme take a whiff." Dylan held the wand up to Claire's nose. "Mmmm, Cotton Candy," Claire said loud enough for Massie to hear. But Massie's face was buried in her game of Breakout. "*Mmmm, Cotton Candy,*" Claire shouted again. "Massie, you'd love this—have a smell."

"Huh?" Massie looked up. Her eyes were tearing, either from the wind or sheer boredom.

"Smell."

Massie leaned forward. She positioned her tiny button nose over the wand and sniffed. Her face came to life like she had just inhaled a bag of smelling salts, then a second later she squinted.

"Nina, am I a used Band-Aid?"

"Uh, no." Nina's eyes were fixed on the soccer players.

"Then why did you rip me off?" Massie's voice was flat and calm, but her teeth were showing, like an attack dog's.

"I have no idea what you're talking about."

"You stole my lip gloss!" Massie yelled.

"Ma'am, I found it!" a referee yelled back from the field.

He was holding up the tube of Taco Belle and waving it between his fingers. He fake-tossed it to let Massie know he was about to throw it. When he actually did, Massie made no effort to catch it, and the stinky gloss plopped down in a muddy puddle just below their feet.

"Where's my crimper? Did you take that too?"

"And what about my bike lock?" Kristen chimed in.

A look of panic washed over Alicia's face, as if she were the one being accused. "Nina, did you take Massie's lip gloss?"

"No!" Nina pouted the way grown-ups do when they want you to think they're offended. "That's crazy talk."

"Then where did you get this?" Massie was shaking the gold tube.

"I bought it at the duty-free shop in the airport." Nina stood up and jumped off the bleacher. She bent down slowly in front of the puddle and picked up the tube of Taco Belle.

"Can we get an instant replay of that?" someone shouted at her from the stands.

Nina bent down again and wiggled her butt. When she straightened back up, the boys in their section applauded. She smiled and waved, then blew another bubble. She looked at Dylan. "Guys love it when you blow big bubbles. It reminds them of boobs."

"Really?" Dylan said. "Lemme have a piece."

"Me too." Kristen forgot all about her missing bike lock.

Nina handed them each a piece of watermelon-flavored Bubblicious, then looked at Massie and scowled. She held the dirty tube over Massie's face so the mud would drip on her face.

"Oops." Nina put her hand over her mouth. "So sorry. I was just trying to show you that your tube is silver and mine is gold. I assumed a rich girl like you would know the difference between the two, but I guess I was wrong."

A teardrop clump of mud slid down Massie's cheek.

"Clean yourself up," Nina instructed. "You're a mess."

Claire felt so uncomfortable for Massie, she could hardly look at her. No one had ever treated her like that before, and it must have been tearing her apart on the inside. But outside she was cool and calm.

"Good idea." Massie unscrewed the top on her bottle of Perrier, shook it, and aimed it at Nina's shirt.

Nina screamed so loud, it sounded like she was getting sprayed with liquid acid, not expensive mineral water. Everyone in their entire section turned to see what had happened. And they loved what they saw. Some of them cheered louder for Nina than they did for the players. After all, the only thing sports fans like more than a good game is a beautiful girl with a pair of D-cups in a soaking wet T-shirt.

Dylan and Kristen stood beside Nina and blew as many big bubbles as they could.

Claire could feel herself starting to panic and silently asked the hearts if Nina would steal Cam away from her. She slowly pulled a green one out of the bag, then ran her finger along its raised letters, hoping to get an idea of what it might say. It was pretty easy to make out the first word; it was *Love.*

Yes! she thought. Everything was going to be okay. She tried to figure out the second word but was having a harder time. There was a *U* and definitely an *S*. It was probably something like *Love Trust* or *Trust Love*, which was good. Claire exhaled and pulled the heart out of the bag. She felt much better, until she flipped it over and read her fortune.

It said, **"Love Hurts."**

"Ten, nine, eight . . ." Massie was shocked by the sound of her own voice counting down the remaining ten seconds of the game. Despite being paralyzed by boredom, she couldn't help getting excited over this last play. Briarwood was ahead by one point, and in seven seconds they would win the playoffs and this game would finally be over.

"Noooo!" Kristen shouted.

"What?" Massie screamed. She didn't know how much more of this she could take.

"Look." She was pointing to some speedy Grayson guy who was kicking the ball toward Derrington. "If he scores, we go into overtime. We could lose."

More importantly, it would mean no MVP pin for Derrington, which would reflect very poorly on her choice of boyfriend.

"Save it!" Massie shouted at Derrington. "Saaa-vvve it!"

"Six, five, four . . ."

Kristen and Claire were squeezing each other's hands, Dylan was blowing her nose, and Nina was shaking her butt in time with the cheerleaders. Alicia didn't stand up until the speedy Grayson guy pulled back his muscular leg, grunted, and kicked the ball. It made a loud popping sound that could be heard over the cheering crowd.

"Three, two . . ."

As the ball shot toward the net, Massie's popularity flashed before her eyes. If Derrington saved this ball, he would be a star and they would be the ahb-vious choice for the Cupid Award. If he didn't . . .

"*Yes!*" Kristen shouted. She grabbed Claire and they both started bouncing up down at the exact same time. They were holding each other so tight, it looked like their torsos had been sewn together.

The Tomahawks punched the cold air with their fists and rushed toward the net. They lifted Derrington above their heads and whooped and hollered like animals. Massie had been too busy thinking about the Cupid Award to catch the actual moment where he'd saved the ball but judging from everyone's reaction, she assumed Derrington had done something right.

A pack of crazed Briarwood fans rushed the field.

"We're going to the playoffs!" Kristen shouted.

"My school in Orlando sucked at sports. It's great to finally be part of the winning team!"

"I'll bet," Dylan mumbled.

Claire leaned across Dylan as if she weren't even there. "Hey, Massie, wanna go on the field and congratulate them?"

Massie suddenly felt overcome by a wave of fear. *What if*

Derrington doesn't like me anymore? What if he wants to be with an older girl or a prettier girl because he's a big soccer star? "Kuh-laire, don't you know anything about boys? Play it cool or you'll look like a fool."

"But they just won—"

"Well, I'm going." Nina put her hands on her hips. "Anyone want to come with me?"

Everyone turned to Massie. She looked at them with a hard stare that double dared them to go with Nina. When no one responded, Nina shrugged her shoulders and ran off alone.

"See, do you want to seem desperate like *her*?" Massie asked Claire.

Claire bit her bottom lip, then shook her head.

"I didn't think so. Now, who needs a touch-up?" Massie reached into her feather clutch and pulled out a suede Coach makeup bag. "The Love Struck dash is in a few minutes. Anyone want some blush?"

No one said a word. They were too busy watching Nina twirl her braids as she spoke to sweaty soccer players. It was obvious from their goofy boyish expressions that they preferred flirting with her to celebrating their victory.

"Guys love her," Kristen sighed.

"How does she do it?" Dylan asked.

"Like this." Massie slammed her blush brush down on the bleacher and stood up. She pushed her small boobs together with her hands, leaned forward, and wiggled her butt.

"Yeah, baby!" an eighth grader shouted.

Massie blew a kiss to her admirer and her friends cracked up. She was back at the center of attention and everything finally felt right again.

"Look," Claire screeched. She was pointing at the field.

Massie's smiled faded.

Nina was standing between Cam and Derrington, with one arm around each of them. The boys seemed completely unaware of the high-fiving and celebrating going on around them. They were too captivated by Nina and what she was saying.

"She's like a snake charmer, only with guys," Dylan said.

"It's ha-zaming!"

"Ehmagod, Alicia," Massie shouted. "Your cousin has G2G!"

"She's probably just congratulating them." Alicia tugged on her braids. "I'm sure it's totally innocent." They watched Nina pat them both on the butt before she sauntered off. "See? She's gone."

"Yeah, but look where she's going now." Claire folded her arms across her chest and looked at Alicia.

"Oh, no, she is *not*." Alicia pulled the rubber bands off her braids and unraveled her hair while Nina handed Josh Hotz a note. He looked like he was about to read it, but Nina put her hand on his and squeezed it, implying that he should wait until he was alone.

"She is so dead to me."

"Maybe you guys are being too hard on her." Dylan pulled the gum from her mouth and twirled it around her index finger. "We should just ask her what we're doing wrong. She can give us a few pointers on how to get boys." She used her teeth to scrape the gum back into her mouth.

Massie squinted her amber eyes and glared at Dylan. "Does it look like we have any trouble with *that*?"

"Uh," Dylan mumbled. "Well, we're up here and they're all down there, so yeah, maybe."

Kristen giggled.

Principal Burns's voice crackled over the loudspeaker, and everyone turned to face the scoreboard. Her face was being broadcast over the Jumbotron like she was the Wizard of Oz.

"Aww, aww!" a guy shouted as soon as her voice came through the speakers. Someone always made crow sounds when Principal Burns spoke, because her beaklike nose and beady black eyes made her look exactly like a bird. As usual, she ignored them.

"Will everyone please clear the field except for the Briarwood Boys?" she asked.

The stadium lights went on, giving everything around them a blinding glow.

It took ten minutes for Principal Burns to get what she had asked for. Finally, when the Briarwood boys were alone on the field, the soccer coach drove around in a golf cart, handing out Velcro suits and forcing the boys to put them on. Massie could hear them moaning in protest from the bleachers. She leaned in toward Claire and whispered, "Aren't you so glad we have a plan? How bad would it suck if we had to chase after a bunch of guys with a bow and arrow like we were desperate or something?"

"I heard that." Kristen was doing the runner's stretch. "Some of us actually have to go through with this." She took a long sip of orange Gatorade.

"At least you know how to run," Dylan whined. "I never learned."

"I can't even walk fast," Alicia put in.

A teacher's aide passed out bows and arrows to the girls in the stands. Once everyone was armed, Principal Burns asked them to stand so she could repeat the rules. But she never had the chance. Everyone stormed the field and the chase was on. Kristen raced down the bleachers, while Alicia and Dylan begged Josh Hotz and Chris Plovert to slow down.

Massie decided to take her time, figuring it was better spent curling her eyelashes and forcing Claire to "put a little color in those pale cheeks."

"Can we go now?" Claire urged. "Pleeeease?" She was squirming and shifting from one foot to the other like she was holding in a massive pee.

"Okay," Massie sighed as she zipped up her makeup bag and dropped it in her purse. "Let's get this over with." She stood up and walked carefully toward the field, trying not to let her heels stick in the grass.

"I don't see them," Claire panicked. "Do you?"

Massie stepped onto the field and looked around. Her classmates were darting past her, hollering like Indians and shooting Velcro-tipped arrows into the air. One by one, boys were getting captured, and the field was slowly starting to clear.

"There they are." Massie pointed. Derrington and Cam were running as quickly as they could toward the far side of the field. None of the other Briarwood Boys seemed half as desperate to escape as they did. "Where are they going?"

"I dunno." Claire looked stunned as she watched them. "*Cam!*" she shouted. "*Caaaam!*"

This time, Massie didn't bother trying to stop Claire from looking desperate. "Call him again," she urged. "Maybe he didn't hear you."

Claire shouted and waved her arms in the air like she was on Park Avenue trying to flag down a cab in the rain. "Over here!"

But the boys kept running.

"Do they think this is funny?" Massie took out her cell phone and speed-dialed Derrington.

"Ugh!" she snapped her phone shut. "Straight to voicemail."

"Maybe they don't think we came to the game?" Claire offered.

"They smiled at us during both halftimes."

"Maybe they're mad because we played hard to get when they won." Claire bit down on her pinky nail, then spit it out on the field. "I knew we should have congratulated them."

Massie considered the same thing but refused to admit

that this was her fault. "No way. Impossible." She looked around the stadium, like she was hoping some sort of explanation would blow by her any minute.

Layne and her two friends Meena and Heather were standing on the sidelines, waving signs that said, OCD GIRLS RUN FOR PRESIDENT, NOT BOYS! and were getting hit with more arrows than the guys.

Dylan was in the distance shooting at Chris Plovert's bad leg, and Alicia was walking behind Josh Hotz trying to figure out how to string her arrow. She was shouting at him, begging him to slow down, but he refused. "At least *try* to run," he shouted back.

"I *am* trying," Alicia insisted as she swung her arms a little faster. "Look!"

But he didn't seem convinced and decided to pick up his pace.

The piercing sound of an air horn punctured the air. "And that's time!" Principal Burns announced.

Massie watched as everyone stood beside their captives with proud sweaty glows on their faces. Kristen was panting beside Kemp Hurley, Dylan was sitting on the cold grass with Chris Plovert, and Nina was surrounded by seven guys, including Eli and Josh Hotz.

"This can't be happening to me," Massie murmured. She ducked down behind the happy couples, grabbed Claire's arm, and pulled her off the field.

"What are you doing?" Claire hissed. "What if they try to find us and explain?"

"There's no way I'm going to stand around completely dateless," Massie said once she had pulled Claire to the parking lot. "I feel naked."

"I don't understand." Claire wiped a tear away from her eyes. "Hearts, why did the boys run away from us?" She pulled out a blue candy, read it, and then whipped it onto the cracked pavement. Massie watched it roll under the front tire of a white Mercedes.

"What did it say?"

"What difference does it make?" Claire pouted. "They're gone." She wiped away another tear. "And so is my first kiss."

At first, Massie couldn't decide what she was more upset about—losing Derrington or missing her shot at the Cupid Award. She searched her mind for an answer, hoping the hollow, empty feeling in her stomach would go away once she figured it out. But it only got worse when she finally did. Because it wasn't all about Derrington and the Cupid Award: it was that Massie Block hadn't come out on top. And there was nothing more devastating than that.

"Massie!" Claire banged on the bathroom door for the third time. "Isaac is honking the horn and I haven't even showered yet. Will you please hurry up?" She loosened the bow on her blue terry cloth robe and contemplated skipping the hygiene thing so they wouldn't be late. But she'd done that yesterday.

"I would have been in here sooner if you hadn't kept me up half the night snoring," Massie shouted over the sound of the water. "You know how hard it is getting out of bed after two hours of sleep?"

Claire leaned forward and yelled at the white high-gloss paint on Massie's bathroom door. "Well, it's not like I slept any better. I can't believe you need to keep the blinds open. The light from the full moon practically scorched my eyelids."

Isaac honked the horn again.

"Massie," Kendra's voice bleated through the intercom, "Isaac has been waiting for ten minutes. Will you please get in the car before the neighbors sue us for noise pollution?"

Claire stepped out of her robe and threw on a fresh pair of jeans and a crisp white long-sleeved T-shirt. At least she would *look* clean.

She padded over to Massie's bay window and stood motionless, watching the workmen scurry around the backyard, some carrying fistfuls of lumber, others hammering and drilling. They were still working on the base of the house, which looked like a big wooden stage. Claire sighed. At this rate, she would be stuck living with Massie until college.

Finally the pipes squeaked and the water stopped running.

Claire laced up her camouflage Converse high-tops and tried not to feel jealous when she heard the breathy scream of Massie's hairdryer. She missed that just-washed feeling and the herbal smell of her shampoo. Claire knew her strawberry-scented oil from the Body Shop was a weak substitution for soap but dabbed a few drops behind her ears anyway. It was all she could do.

The low farting sound of Todd's tuba seeped through the walls. Claire clenched her fists a little tighter with every off-key blast.

Massie stepped out of the bathroom. "What is this?" She was holding a tiny black object that was no bigger than a button. An avalanche of steam followed her. "I found it in the shower."

Claire walked toward her and plucked the mysterious item out of Massie's palm. The instant she saw it, she knew what it was, and her heart started racing. "I dunno. I can't think with that tuba blasting in the other room. I'm going to tell Todd to stop. I'll be in the car."

"Did you just say you'll bring Bean back?" Massie asked.

"No. I said I'll *be in* the car."

"Oh."

Claire scooped up her backpack, stomped next door to Todd's room, and barged in without knocking. Her brother was standing on his bed in a pair of SpongeBob SquarePants boxers, watching himself play tuba in the mirror.

"Is this one of your cameras?" Claire shouted in a whisper.

Todd ignored her and kept playing.

She kicked the leg of his bed. "One blast for yes, two for no."

Puuuurp

"Todd, you can't hide cameras in Massie's shower. That's beyond perverted, and it's illegal."

Puuurp

She could see the corners of his mouth curling up. He was trying not to laugh.

"If I find anymore spy gear, I'm telling Mom," Claire said. "And the police."

Puuurp, puuurp.

"Yes, I am!" Claire stormed out of his room.

Isaac started honking again as she ran down the stairs.

"Claire," Judi shouted from the kitchen. *"Hurry up!"*

"I say let them be late," Kendra said. "It's the only way they'll learn."

Claire stood outside the kitchen and listened.

"I can't just ignore this, Kendra." Judi sounded upset. "Tardiness is a bad habit."

"I know, dear, but they're growing up, and they have to learn to make their own mistakes." Kendra's white coffee cup made a clinking sound as she set it down on the matching china saucer.

"Where I come from, mistakes are things like adding two cups of sugar when the recipe calls for one. *Not* letting my daughter develop a reputation for being disrespectful," Judi said.

"Are you saying I encourage Massie to be disrespectful?"

"Are you saying you don't?"

"Uh, good morning." Claire forced a smile. "Massie will be right down. She's really upset about being late; she just has a terrible stomachache.

Kendra smirked at Judi. "Is she okay? Does she want to stay home?"

Massie hurried into the kitchen. She was cradling Bean in her arms. "No, I'm feeling much better." She thanked Claire silently with her eyes. "Let's go." She pressed her finger into one of the points on her gold star brooch that was pinned to the side of her navy blue cashmere cowl-neck. The color of the sweater reminded Claire of the night sky. She yawned and rubbed her tired, burning eyes.

Massie opened the front door, bent down, and picked up her latest delivery of Glossip Girl. She tore open the brown box on her way to the car and read the label on the silver tube. "Ew." She whipped it into the back of the workmen's pickup truck.

"What was it?" Claire asked as she slid across the backseat of the Range Rover.

"Baby's Breath." Massie made a disgusted face as she pulled the seat belt across her lap and clicked it in the buckle.

"You didn't even open it."

"Why would I? It probably smells like spit-up."

Claire didn't bother telling Massie that Baby's Breath was a type of flower. It was payback for not being able to shower for two days in a row.

"No talking," Isaac snapped as he pulled out of the Blocks' circular driveway. "I have a terrible headache from honking that horn all morning."

"Sorry Isaa—"

"Claire." He turned around and looked her in the eye. "I said no talking."

Massie giggled, then turned to face the window. He told Alicia, Nina, Dylan, and Kristen the same thing when he picked them up. For the first time in carpool history, the girls rode to school in complete silence.

When Isaac stopped the silver Range Rover in front of the school, they were ten minutes late. Massie kicked open the door with her foot and jumped onto the pavement. She was gasping for air.

"I almost asphyxiated on your cheap perfume," she spat

at Nina. "The bottle should come with a childproof cap and a number for the poison control hotline."

Claire and Alicia laughed. Dylan and Kristen looked at Nina with sympathy.

"Go to class," Isaac shouted before screeching out of the parking lot.

The girls strolled up the main stairs of OCD and ducked when they passed Principal Burns's window.

When they were safely inside, Massie whispered to Kristen and Dylan, "What are you two wearing?" They stopped walking and looked at their own outfits, then glanced at Nina.

"Did you put them up to this?" Massie started walking again. Then everyone else did too.

"*Sí.* I think they look sexy." Nina bent down and fluffed the pink pom-poms on her red suede knee-high boots.

"Sexy?" Massie turned to Nina. "Look at Dylan's makeup. It looks like she spent the morning making out with a clown."

"Danks ha lot, Bassie." Dylan sneezed. "I tink it looks good. I need a little color on my face 'cause I've been doh sick." She blew her nose and examined the tissue. It was covered in red lipstick and orange foundation.

"Gross!" Alicia laughed.

"And Kristen, I don't know what's worse—that tacky pink Wet Seal V-neck or the C-cups poking out of it." Massie looked away in horror.

Claire couldn't help laughing. It looked like Kristen's boobs were being smothered against their will.

"It's a Victoria's Secret water bra." Kristen adjusted her cleavage by squeezing her arms together and squirming around. "Nina said it would make me feel more feminine, you know, while my hair grows out."

"Don't tell me," Massie said to Alicia. "You're wearing a garter belt under your Frankie B.'s, right?"

"No." Alicia looked upset that Massie had even suggested such a thing.

"I tried to get her to wear a micromini because she has such long legs, but she was too afraid of what Mayssie would say." Nina made a baby face when she said, "Mayssie."

Massie looked at Alicia with a pleased grin. Alicia humbly returned it.

"Maybe you three should wear Sage's Virgins for Life shirts." Nina burst out laughing at her own joke. Her shrill cackle echoed through the empty halls.

"Why aren't you girls in class?" Principal Burns shouted from the other end of the hall.

"Uh, sorry we're late," Kristen apologized politely. "W-we had car trouble."

"Do you have a note?"

"Laaaaaahhh," Nina sang. "That note was D minor."

Dylan was the only one who giggled.

Principal Burns put her hands on her hips and tapped

her sensible rubber-soled winter boot against the freshly waxed floors.

"Now I have something for you. It also starts with D. It's called a detention. And you'll serve it now, during first period."

Kristen gasped. "But that counts as an absence," she said. "And my scholarship only lets me have—"

"You should have thought of that when you were moseying down the hall at 8:45 A.M.," said Principal Burns. "Now go to room six while I notify your parents."

"No, please don't," Kristen pleaded. "My mom will freak."

But all they heard were the squeaky rubber soles of Principal Burns's boots as she hurried back to her office.

"I am so grounded." Kristen ran her hand against the lockers while they walked. "I bet my mother says I can't go to the dance."

"Really?" Dylan's face lit up. "Nina, does that mean I automatically win the bet?"

"Yup."

"Oh, you're a good friend," Kristen snapped.

"This is for three pairs of boots," Dylan said. "It has nothing to do with friendship."

"Well, I'll dig a tunnel with a spoon and crawl to the dance if I have to. Because I'm not going to let you beat me."

Dylan puckered up and chased Kristen down the hall with her germ-infested lips. "Come 'ere, sexy—I can't resist your water bra."

The door to room six seemed to open on its own when the girls arrived. But Mrs. Peckish was on the other side, resting one of her wrinkled, veiny hands on the knob and running the other through her unruly shoulder-length white hair. She was wearing a giant misshapen puke-green sweater. It swallowed up her tiny frame.

"Welcome." She sounded like a witch in a haunted house. "You will spend the next thirty minutes in silence staring into my tired old eyes, thinking about what you have done to deserve this." She was brewing a pot of black coffee that made the whole room smell bitter.

Mrs. Peckish was so frail and creepy that Claire wondered if maybe OCD had been built on her grave and she had come back to haunt it.

The girls sat in a straight line across the back row of seats and stared at Mrs. Peckish like they were told. It was the first time Claire had even seen bare walls in a classroom. No maps, flags, or posters of Einstein, just a peeling layer of pus-yellow paint and a chalkboard.

A cold draft blew through the room, and Claire stuck her icy hands under her armpits for warmth. She looked at the open window, then at Mrs. Peckish. The teacher smiled kindly, walked over to the window, and opened it even more.

Dylan sneezed.

"Can I get a Kleenex?" She pinched her nose.

"No," Mrs. Peckish snapped. "You stay here. I'll get it."

The minute she left the room, the girls started whispering.

"You better take care of that cold," Nina instructed. "You don't want to be sick for the dance."

"I doh." Dylan sniffed. "Do you doh who you're going with yet?"

"I couldn't decide between Josh, Cam, and Derringtons," Nina said. "So they are all going to take me."

"You're lying," Massie barked.

"I am not. They certainly didn't run away from me."

Claire clenched her fist and waited for Massie to jump in with a cutting remark. But she didn't. In fact, Massie didn't say anything at all. She just stared at Nina with her squinted amber eyes and slowly shook her head.

"FYI, Josh wasn't running away from me—he was just running, period," Alicia said. "And I simply don't do that."

"Hey, you three should join in on our bet. It will be nuf."

Before anyone could answer, Dylan flipped her hair and said, "Oh, I could never do a thing like that. My name is Claire and I want my first kiss to be romaaaaantic."

Claire couldn't believe Dylan was throwing that back in her face.

Kristen and Nina laughed.

"I'll still get my kiss," Claire insisted. "You'll see." She bit down on her thumbnail.

"Silence." Mrs. Peckish came back into the room. "Look at me."

A few seconds later Claire felt her cell phone vibrating in her back pocket. She managed to keep her eyes locked on Mrs. Peckish while she pulled it out. When the witch turned around to pour herself another cup of coffee, Claire read the message.

MASSIE: N is so done. Must get revenge.

Claire couldn't type without looking at her screen like Massie could, so she looked over and nodded her head to show that she agreed.

MASSIE: A is on board.

Alicia kept her face forward but shifted her big brown eyes toward Claire. Claire nodded again.

MASSIE: Lemme think of plan.

This time Claire didn't nod in agreement. Instead she looked down at her swollen cuticles and imagined how satisfying it would be if she were the one to hatch the evil plan, not Massie. Ever since Nina had come to town, Cam had stopped talking to her. No more mix CDs, love letters, or candy. Now she would never get to kiss him at the dance. She was tired of crying herself to sleep over Cam and brushing it off as snoring. It was time to take action.

CLAIRE: I have flan.

She managed to type without looking.

Massie shot her a confused look and must have forwarded the message, because Alicia giggled.

"Hey!" Mrs. Peckish made a peace sign with her fingers and then turned it on its side so it looked like she was poking herself in the eyes with it. The girls did what they were told until the teacher reached into her purse to search for her bag of sunflower seeds.

MASSIE: U really have plan?

Claire nodded and held up her palm to show that she swore by it. Operation Toe Jam was something she'd done with her girlfriends back in Orlando when they wanted to flirt. But with a few tweaks, it could be used to bring Nina down. And Claire knew that would give Massie a good enough reason to like her again.

The lunch bell rang and the classroom doors flew open, giving way to hordes of hungry girls racing to be first in line at the Café.

Claire checked her pink Baby G-Shock watch. It was exactly 12:15 P.M. That gave her one minute to meet up with Massie on the library steps, ten minutes to get supplies, three to be in position, and one to give Alicia the signal. If Operation Toe Jam was a success, Claire would be too. And if not . . .

Claire shook the thought from her head.

As planned, Massie was waiting on the library steps, flipping through an issue of *Teen Vogue*.

"Cheers, Big Ears." Massie jumped to her feet.

"Same goes, Big Nose." Claire was relieved that most of the tension from the morning had melted away. Banding together against Nina certainly had its benefits.

"Do you think we can make it there and back in ten minutes?" Claire's eyes were fixed on the 7-Eleven across the street.

"If we run." Massie pointed to her feet. She was wearing a pair of black-and-gold Reeboks. It was the first time Claire had ever seen her in sneakers outside of gym class.

"Where did you—?"

"I snuck into the locker room during English," Massie announced.

"Nice. Let's go."

The girls managed to make it across the street before the yellow light turned red, which put them right on schedule.

When they got to 7-Eleven, Claire pushed the door open and bolted straight to the bubble gum section. Massie was close behind her.

"This always worked at my old school," Claire panted, "so I'm pretty sure it will work here."

Claire had never thought she'd see the day when Massie Block and Alicia Rivera agreed to follow *her* plan, and it was making her nervous. She silently asked the hearts if this mission would be a success, then reached into her front pocket and pulled out a pink piece of candy. It said, **"Be Mine."** Claire had no idea how to interpret that and concluded that the hearts could only answer questions about love.

"I don't see it," Massie snapped. "And we only have three minutes left."

"There it is," Claire shouted. "Over by the wax lips." She grabbed four packages of grape-flavored Big League Chew off the rack and sniffed them. Her stomach sank. "This smell reminds me of Cam. BLC is his favorite gum."

Massie grabbed the packages out of Claire's hand. "Stay

focused," she snapped as she marched to the counter and paid with a crisp fifty-dollar bill.

"Do you think Cam and Derrington are really going to the dance with Nina?" Claire asked as they ran across the street. "Is it really possible? What did we do wrong?"

Once they were back on OCD property, Massie stopped running. She waited to catch her breath before she spoke.

"Claire, do I spend eight hours a day sitting at a big round desk in the middle of the mall?"

"No."

"Then why do you think I have the information?"

Massie smiled sweetly, maybe to let Claire know she wasn't trying to be mean. Claire returned the smile. She felt silly for thinking Massie had all the answers, especially since she was probably asking herself the same questions about Derrington.

"One thing I do know is that Nina had eh-verything to do with it." Massie slipped on her brown suede heels and stuffed her sneakers in the hot pink fur-lined bag on her shoulder. "So let's get that wuss in boots."

Claire followed Massie up the main steps and into the school. Even though it was Claire's plan, she was relieved to see Massie taking charge again. It took some of the pressure off.

It was 12:30 P.M. when they arrived at their stakeout spot behind the Dasani vending machine, outside the Café. It was time for Alicia's lunchtime news announcement and the beginning of Operation Toe Jam. They were right on schedule.

Bon appetit, OCD. This is Alicia Rivera with your lunchtime news brief.

Everyone in the halls stopped moving and looked up at the speakers in the corners of the ceiling.

A string of mysterious robberies has left a few of our students rattled this morning. The first crime was reported on Friday by Jessi Rowan, who noticed the furry monkey key chain on her Kipling backpack was gone. Several more reports have come in today. Among the list of missing items are Natalie Nussbaum's Chococat pencil case, Mrs. Beeline's red Montblanc pen, and my Ralph Lauren argyle gym socks. Think twice before leaving open lockers unattended, and please report any suspicious activity to Principal Burns . . . . This has been Alicia Rivera for OCD news saying, I heart you.

The usual amount of applause followed and everyone returned to their previous conversations.

Alicia finished at exactly 12:40 P.M., right on schedule. Massie reached into her back pocket for her cell phone and accidentally elbowed Claire in the ribs.

"Sorry," she whispered. "It's just so cramped back here."

Claire mouthed, "It's okay."

After Massie sent Alicia a text message saying that they were ready, Claire gave the order to start chewing.

Claire and Massie tore open the bags of BLC and stuffed handfuls of the purple shredded gum in their mouths.

Massie held her hand over her mouth to keep the gum from falling out and when she moved it away, it was covered in spit. She wiped it on the side of the vitamin water machine and went right back to chewing.

"Ew." Claire started laughing so hard, she almost choked . . . until she heard the slow whine of the electronic dollar-bill taker. Knowing someone was standing on the other side of the machine made her freeze with fear. Claire's mouth was overflowing with spit from the wad of gum she was chewing. But she was too afraid to make even the slightest swallowing sound, so she dropped her jaw and let the excess saliva dribble onto the ground. Surprisingly enough, Massie did the same thing. And the girls' bodies shook with suppressed laughter.

The machine whined again.

"This thing sucks," someone said before kicking it three times.

Massie yelped and then covered her mouth.

"Kori, did you hear something?"

It was Strawberry, the violent redhead that Alicia had recruited to replace Dylan when they were fighting last semester.

"Like a puppy getting stepped on?" Kori offered.

"Yeah."

Claire felt a rush of sweat to her armpits. She would definitely need a shower tomorrow.

"Maybe there's an animal stuck in the machine and that's why it's broken," Kori suggested.

The girls giggled and walked away.

Massie and Claire sighed with relief.

Uh, excuse me? I have one more announcement. . . .

Everyone stopped again when they heard Alicia's voice.

Will Nina Callas please come to the DJ booth ASAP for a very important message? This has been Alicia Rivera for OCD news saying, I heart you.

As soon as they heard that, Claire and Massie started pulling chunks of purple gum out of their mouths and whipping them onto the floor. The familiar click-clacking of Nina's boots echoed through the empty halls as she tore out of the Café to meet Alicia in the DJ booth.

"Music to my ears." Claire smiled. Everything was going as planned.

The louder the click-clacking got, the more they chewed and tossed. Unfortunately, a group of Frankenstein-boot-wearing drama geeks who were skipping down the halls singing "Popular" from the Broadway musical *Wicked* happened to stumble through the purple minefield before Nina did. Despite Massie's audible cackle, they didn't notice.

Finally Nina rounded corner. Claire was so nervous, she buried her face in Massie's shoulder. "Did she step in it yet?"

"Not yet," Massie whispered. "Oh, wait. . . . Nope . . . Oh . . . There she goes. . . . A little to the left . . . *Yes!*"

Claire lifted her head.

"*Dios!*" Nina shouted as she scraped the bottom of one boot against the top of the other, which only made it worse. Now there was gum smeared across the toes of her red suede boots. "*Ayudar.*" She looked around the halls. "Help!"

When no one came, Nina dropped to the floor, crossed her legs, and tried her best to pull the gum off. But her long nails made it difficult to get a grip. Eventually, she managed to scrape most of it off her left boot, but the right one was too far gone.

"No. *Dios*, no!" she moaned, upon discovering a wad tangled around the pink pom-poms and stuck in the rear zipper tracks.

"Mission accomplished," Claire whispered. "She's nothing without those boots."

"It's like we captured the broomstick of the wicked witch," Massie said quietly.

After a good amount of grunting and groaning, Nina managed to pull off her boot. She started weeping softly, cradling it like a kitten that had just fallen out of a tree.

"That's your cue. Go! Good luck."

Claire slid out from behind the vending machine and walked toward Nina as if she were enjoying a casual lunchtime stroll down the hall.

"Nina, is that you sitting alone on the floor?" Claire tilted her head as she approached, in a show of genuine concern. She hoped Massie would appreciate her convincing delivery.

Nina looked up. Black streaks of mascara and smudges of blue eyeliner had skidded into the red circles of rouge on her cheeks. Her face looked like a melted oil painting.

"My boots are ruined." She lifted her legs into the air so Claire could see for herself.

"Yeah, you gotta be careful in these halls," Claire pointed out. "They can be hard to navigate, especially in ridiculously high heels, like those."

Nina sniffed, then wiped her nose with her wrist.

Claire felt a pang of guilt. Could she really go through with this? She knew what it felt like to be the hated "new girl" and was finding it hard to humiliate someone the way the Pretty Committee used to humiliate her. She would just tell Massie and Alicia that Nina had run off to the bathroom and ruined the rest of the plan. Seconds after making this decision, Claire felt her shoulders relax. The guilt was gone.

"Nina," Claire suggested in her kindest voice, "why don't you go to the bath—?"

But Nina ignored her. Instead she pushed herself up off the ground and faced Claire. She was at least two inches taller, even without the boots. "I can't wear these to Briarwood after school. They're disgusting."

"Briarwood?" Claire asked.

"*Sí*, Cam and Derringtons are going to give me a private tour of the boys' locker room."

"You don't say." Claire clenched her fists together and stuffed them in the front pockets of her Old Navy jeans.

"Well, then, I have the perfect solution." She was back to the original plan. Only this time there was no guilt whatsoever. "Let's go to Nurse Adele's office. She has a lost and found that is more stocked than Bloomingdale's. She'll definitely have spare boots."

"But will they be sexy?" Nina asked. "And high? How high will they be?"

"She'll have whatever you need," Claire said. "Follow me."

"What about designer name brands?"

Claire clenched her fists again and took a long deep breath. "She has it all."

"Good. Because everyone expects me to look fabulous."

"Of course they do," Claire said as she passed one of Layne's NINA IS OBSCENA posters.

"Don't you just love those?" Nina admired Layne's work.

"They don't upset you?"

"No." Nina chuckled. "There is no such thing as bad press."

Claire wondered what it would actually take to break this girl. She was harder to destroy than pleather.

After a short walk down the hall, the girls arrived at the nurse's office. It was the only white door in the school, with lace curtains in the window instead of the standard beige metal blinds.

"Wait here on the bench," Claire said. "It's better if I go in and get what she has—you know, 'cause we're friends and everything."

Nina shrugged her shoulders and sat down on the wooden bench that was pressed up against the wall outside the office. The only people that ever sat on it were kids with lice who were waiting for their parents to pick them up. Claire hoped that people would pass by and assume Nina's hair was an infested nest.

After a quick chat about flu shots with Nurse Adele, Claire excused herself and went to the lost-and-found closet. For some reason, the boot selection was better than ever, which was exactly what Claire didn't want. She ignored the silver Sigerson Morrison kitten heels and let her eyes drift past the cute red leather cowboy boots. Instead she grabbed a pair of stinky brown Birkenstocks that had probably belonged to Sage. Then she picked up one of every ugly shoe that came in a size six.

Nina already had her boots off in anticipation of the new designer boots she'd be trying on. She was massaging her feet when Claire walked out of Nurse Adele's office.

"Here you go," Claire announced with the pride of a Foot Locker salesman who had just emerged from the stock-room with a wonderful selection. She dropped the shoes in a heap at Nina's feet.

"What is this?" Nina lifted up a black-and-white-checkered sneaker that had a ketchup stain on the toe. "No. *Dios!*" She dropped it as if it were covered in roaches.

"That shoe is popular with the skater crowd. It's called a Van." Claire searched her messy pile of shoes. "Here you go." She lifted up a black pump. "I would pair it with this Cynthia Rowley dress shoe, because of the similar colors."

"But they are two completely different styles," Nina gasped. She leaned over and started sifting through the pile herself. "None of these match."

"These do." Claire held up the Birkenstocks.

Nina winced as she unbuckled the side strap and slid her foot inside. Claire's insides were trembling with suppressed laughter. She hated that Massie and Alicia weren't there to witness this. Why should she have all the fun?

Nina shuffled across the floor like an old lady in a nursing home. "Too big."

She kicked them off and reached for the Van/pump combination. This time she hobbled across the floor, and Claire burst out laughing.

"Sorry. It's just that they're so, uh . . . big."

"I know. And I like my things to fit."

"I've noticed," Claire mumbled. "But I grabbed you a size six, same as the boots you wore at the sleepover."

"Maybe a size six in America is different than it is in Spain," Nina countered. "Like in Westchester a six is really a five."

Nina managed to find one silver pump that she liked and a similar gold one. She pulled a pair of Ralph Lauren argyle socks out of her bag and slid them on over her fishnet stockings. Then she stepped into the shoes. They fit perfectly.

As they walked down the hall, everyone stared at Nina's feet. Claire couldn't help filling up with pride. She'd done it. She'd actually come up with a plan that would show everyone how lame Nina really was.

Eventually, the whispers turned into pointing. While they walked, Claire snuck a peek at Nina to see if she was starting to sense the negative attention. But if she was, she showed no signs of it. Her head was held high and her strides were long and confident despite the two different heels.

Finally the ultra-stylish Sydney Applebaum and her best friend, Emma Levy, approached Nina. Claire could hardly control her excitement. She wanted to remember everything so she could tell Massie and Alicia everything without missing one humiliating detail.

"Cool shoes, Nina," Sydney said.

"Totally. *J'adore* the two different colors," said her best friend, Emma. "Could you be any more fashion-forward?"

"*Gracias.*" Nina smiled and waved. "Glad you like them." She admired her own feet.

"We totally have to go to shopping in Spain this summer," Sydney said to Emma as they passed by.

Claire rolled her eyes.

The après-lunch bell rang and the halls started filling up again.

"Thanks for your help, Claire." Nina waved goodbye.

"Where are you going?" Claire asked. "Don't you have fifth period?"

"*Sí,* but I have to go to the DJ booth to see what my cousin wanted."

"Oh yeah." Claire moped back to her locker, wondering how she would explain to Massie and Alicia that she'd helped Nina start a new trend.

"Claire Lyons?" Principal Burns crowed.

"Yes?" Claire turned around. She had never heard the principal say her name before.

"I have a report saying that you and Miss Block spent your lunch hour hiding behind a vending machine, stealing dollar bills. Is that true?"

Claire felt a wave of dizziness, like she was slipping into a wavy TV dream sequence.

"Uh, no. We weren't stealing money."

"Well, that's not what I heard," Principal Burns said. "Everyone is starting to say that you and Massie may be the cat burglars."

"But that's not—"

"Either way, you and Miss Block will have another detention after school. And that's final." Principal Burns turned on her rubber heels and squeaked off down the hall.

When Claire arrived in Mrs. Peckish's room after school, it was colder than it had been that morning. And instead of bitter coffee, everything smelled like egg. Claire shivered in her seat, wondering if Strawberry and Kori were responsible for this.

The door flew open and Massie strutted in with a grin on her face. Claire loved Massie's ability to make detention seem like something she'd chosen for herself.

"Strawberry and Kori," Massie mouthed to Claire as she took her seat.

Bing, bang, bong.

The announcement bell sounded over the loudspeaker.

"Will all staff please report to the teachers' lounge for an emergency faculty meeting," said Principal Burns.

Mrs. Peckish sighed then shrugged. "That's me," she said. "You two better be here when I get back."

"We will." Massie tried to sound as sweet as possible.

After the door clicked shut, Claire turned to Massie. "Will it bother you if I take a shower tonight? I need to wash this day off of me."

"Go right ahead. If you promise to pick your clothes up off the floor, I might even let you take one tomorrow."

"Really?" Claire joked, even though she was serious.

"Yup." Massie's eyes drifted off for a second. "Hey, I'll make you a deal."

Claire turned to face Massie.

"If you let Bean come back in the room, I'll let you take first shower every day."

"But it wasn't my idea to get rid of her—it was your mom's," Claire insisted. She couldn't believe they were back on the Bean topic again.

"Well, what if you tell her it really was a cold after all?" Massie suggested. "And for the rest of the week, you'll sleep in the bathtub."

"What?"

"I'll fill it with sleeping bags and cashmere blankets, and you can have all of my down pillows except for one."

Claire tapped the bottom of her chin with a Bic pen. The more she thought about it, the less crazy it seemed. Not only would she be able to shower again, but she could sleep in darkness and cry about Cam as loud as she wanted.

"Deal."

They stuck out their hands to shake but quickly drew them back when the door flew open. Claire and Massie turned and faced the front of the room and folded their hands on their desks.

"It's just me," Kristen moped. Her pink Wet Seal V-neck was splattered with what looked like french fry grease. And she looked utterly exhausted, as if the pressures of life had finally managed to beat her down.

"What are you doing here?" Massie whispered.

"I got too close to the Bunsen burner in science class and my water bra exploded. Do you know they're actually filled with oil and not water?"

Claire and Massie started cracking up.

"It's not funny." Kristen wiped her eyes. "My mother is going to kill me."

"Why should you get in trouble for burning your bra?" Claire asked. "It was an accident."

"Well, that part was but the rest wasn't," Kristen added. "I had hot oil dripping down my chest, so I took off the bra under my shirt and threw it across the room."

Even Kristen laughed at herself this time.

"Ladies, what's all the ruckus about?"

The girls faced forward and stopped laughing immediately.

"Relax," Dylan said. "It's just me." Her face looked like she had dipped it in a bowl of melted Skittles.

"What are *you* doing here?" Kristen looked disgusted.

"I kept sneezing in art, and every time I blew my nose my makeup would come off," she explained.

"So?" the girls said.

"So, Vincent caught be rubbing a green pastel on by eyelids and a red one on by lips." She tried to blow her stuffed-up nose, but nothing came out.

Kristen slammed her hands down on her desk. "Aren't pastels poisonous?"

"Vincent seems to think they are," Dylan said. "That's why I'm here."

"Hey, guys." Alicia sounded bubbly when she walked into the room.

"No way!" Massie clapped her hands.

"What did *you* do?" Dylan asked.

"Nothing," Alicia said.

"Then why are you here?" Claire asked.

"Because everyone else is." Alicia strolled over to the empty desk beside Massie and slowly lowered herself into the seat. "Plus it's the first chance I've had to get away from Nina since she moved here. She keeps talking about the new trend she's started in footwear. It's so ah-nnoying."

Alicia glared at Claire, obviously blaming her for Nina's latest success.

"Sorry," Claire sighed.

"Why?" Massie asked. "What happened?"

"Nothing," Claire murmured.

"She's right about that," Alicia said. "We're right back where we started. The only thing Operation Toe Jam did to Nina was make her more popular."

Normally, Claire would have defended herself. But she couldn't. Alicia was right.

"Kuh-laire, *what happened*?" Massie asked again.

"Silence!" Mrs. Peckish clapped her hands as she walked back into the classroom. "I want silence."

Luckily for Claire, that was exactly what she got.

Massie leaned against the thick wooden door inside the school, pushed it open, and stepped into the OCD parking lot. "Free at last!" She lifted her arms and spun around. The wide bell sleeves on her purple wool coat let in the cold air and stung her bare arms.

An ah-nnoying car horn was honking in the distance, but Massie didn't care. She was just so happy to be out of that stinky detention room. "Here's Isaac." She pointed at the round headlights on the Range Rover as it pulled into the lot. "Who wants to go shopping for dresses? The Love Struck dance is three days away, and if I'm going solo, I have to look ah-mazing."

"I can't believe I'm going alone," Claire mumbled, looking at the cracked asphalt, slowly shaking her head.

"I can't believe *Massie Block* is going alone." Kristen shook her head. "What if everyone thinks you're a loser?"

"They won't when they hear my new philosophy on school dances."

"What philosophy?" Kristen asked.

"You gotta be single to mingle!" Massie shouted.

Claire and Alicia hollered their support. Massie lifted her palm in the air and the girls exchanged high fives.

The mysterious horn was still honking.

Dylan lowered herself onto the curb and sat down. Her forehead was beaded with sweat and her voice was weak. "Don't pretend you're excited to be dateless."

"Who's pretending?" Massie asked

The noisy horn finally stopped. A slamming car door and the sound of heels clacking on the pavement took its place.

"Dylan, do you think we're going to look like losers because we have dates?" Kristen asked.

Dylan shrugged and rested her cheek on the frozen ground.

"What are you doing?"

"Cooling off," Dylan moaned. "It must be two hundred degrees out tonight." The bright headlights on the Range Rover shone in her face as Isaac pulled up along the curb. "Look how strong the sun is. We should be indoors."

The girls started giggling.

"We're you waiting long?" Isaac asked as he held the door open for Massie.

"About a half-hour," she lied. "But I won't tell Mom if you take us to the mall."

"Don't you have homework?"

"We finished it in detention." Massie slid across the leather seats.

"Well, no daughter of mine is going shopping after a detention!" a woman shouted.

Kristen turned and looked over her shoulder. "Mom?"

Massie opened her window so she could hear better.

"That's right." Mrs. Gregory was clenching the wooden cross on her necklace.

Massie leaned across Claire and stuck her head out the window so she wouldn't miss a thing. Kristen's mom looked the same as always, wiry gray roots spreading across the top of her mousy brown bob. Her bangs were heavy and cut straight across her forehead like Buster Brown's and her facial features were small and plain.

"When did you get here?" Kristen had one foot inside the Range Rover and one on the ground.

"I came as soon as I heard about your striptease in science class." Mrs. Gregory sounded mad. "I've been honking for the last fifteen minutes."

Dylan lifted her head off the pavement and giggled like a drunk. "Mrs. Gregory's a goose. She honks!" She fell back down.

Mrs. Gregory let go of her cross and bent down toward Dylan. "Is she on drugs?"

"NyQuil," Dylan slurred, and then giggled again.

Isaac adjusted his black leather driving gloves, then crouched down. After a few manly grunts, he managed to lift Dylan over his shoulder, like a fireman. He used his free hand to open the back hatch, then spread her out across the very backseat.

"Let's go, Kristen Michelle. Your father is waiting to talk to you."

"Lehp," Kristen muttered as she lowered her foot onto

the ground. She waved goodbye slowly and then followed her mother to their fuel-efficient Chrysler.

"Mrs. Gregory sucks," Alicia said as she stepped into the Range Rover.

"Does this bean I win da bet?" Dylan called from the backseat. She sounded delirious. "Are we at the ball yet?"

"You're not going to the mall." Isaac started the engine. "I'm taking you home."

Dylan started laughing hysterically. "Where did all of these pink snakes come from? And why are they wearing swim goggles?" Then she began to weep. "Those are my goggles. *Mine!*"

Isaac stepped on the gas and sped all the way to Dylan's house. He carried her up the thirty stone steps that led to the front door of their mansion and left her in the tender care of her housekeeper, Flora.

"I can't believe she would go to school with the flu," he said when he got back in the car.

"She hates missing out." Massie shook her head. "She's been like that forever."

Isaac reached in the glove compartment and took out a pack of Lysol hand wipes. He cleaned his gloves and the steering wheel, then handed some to the girls so they could disinfect the backseat. "Where to next?" he asked.

"The Westchester Mall," Alicia announced

"Massie?" Isaac waited for her to give the final approval.

"The Westchester!"

Alicia bounced up and down in her seat and clapped.

"Hey, did you guys know that shoe sizes are different in Europe than they are in Westchester?" Claire put in.

"What?" Alicia asked.

"Yeah, like a six there is really a five here," Claire explained. "Cause when I took Nina to try on all the shoes, none of the sixes fit her. They were all too big."

"So maybe she's a five," Massie said. "Who cares?"

"But during the sleepover she *told* us her boots were a six," Claire insisted. "Don't you remember when Kristen and Dylan tried them on at the sleepover? They're both fives, and the boots were way too big for them."

"Gawd, *CSI* much?"

"I'm just wondering why she would lie about the size of her feet?"

"It's so funny that Nina is even into boots," Alicia pointed out. "She used to be such a dorky dresser. She was even worse than—" She looked at Claire. "I mean, she used to wear jellies and socks to restaurants."

"Ew," Massie said.

"Her sisters were the ones who were into footwear. They're, like, famous for their style. Everyone copies them, and twice a year they auction off last season's boots and use the cash to buy more. They raised enough money last year to fly to Paris and shop there."

"Maybe that's why they keep calling." Massie smiled. "Maybe Nina stole their boots, just like she stole my lip gloss."

"And my boyfriend," Claire sneered.

"No, wait—you might be onto something." Alicia's brown eyes were wide with wonder. "Whenever I get back from Spain, I'm always missing a few of my favorite things. But I always blamed the baggage handlers at the airline. But what if it was Nina all this time? What if she's a *gato* burglar?"

"I can totally see that." Massie unclipped her seat belt and sat forward.

"Me too." Claire nodded. "Totally."

"Plan." Alicia pulled her cell out of the inside pocket of her gray coat and started thumbing through her received calls. "I still have her sisters' number stored in here. Should I call and ask if they're missing anything?"

"Yeah!" Massie and Claire said at the same time.

Massie leaned forward and lowered the radio. Alicia dialed and then hit speaker phone.

They squeezed each other's hands while they waited for someone to answer. The ring sounded different, more like a piercing beep.

Boop, boop . . . Boop, boop . . .

"Hey, Alicia, are you in love with your cousins?" Massie asked.

"Huh?" Alicia whispered. "No."

Boop, boop . . .

"Then why are you making a booty call?" Massie cracked up at her own joke.

Alicia and Claire started laughing too.

Boop, boop . . . Boop, boop . . .

"Maybe they're eating dinner," Claire whispered.

Alicia shrugged.

"*Hola?*" a sleepy voice finally answered.

"Uh, *hola.* It's Alicia. Your, uh, *prima.* Is this Celia?"

"*Sí,*" the voice whispered softly. Celia sounded like she was scrunched up in a ball.

"Are you . . . Uh, *estás enferma?*" Alicia said.

"*No, estoy durmiendo.*"

Alicia shrugged.

"Sleeping," Claire whispered. "I think *durmiendo* means *sleeping.*"

Alicia checked her Tiffany watch, then covered the speaker on the phone with her hand and mouthed, "It's only five in the evening."

"I think they're like seven hours ahead," Massie said. "I realized that when I was trying to preorder a Balenciaga bag from the head offices in Spain. They were never open when I called."

Alicia covered her mouth with her hand and gasped. "Ooops."

Claire and Massie giggled.

"*Hola? Hola?*"

"Excuse me," Alicia apologized into the phone. "I'm here . . . Uh, *estoy aqui. La razón* I am, uh, calling is, uh—"

"Lemme try," Claire whispered. She leaned closer to the phone. "*Hola,* Celia, *mi nombre es* Claire. Are you missing any *zapatos?*"

"*Sí!*" Celia sprang to life. "*Quien es? Eres tu la ladrona maldita que levantes mis botas? La policía te van encontrar, y cuando te encuentren, te vam amatar!*"

"Uh, okay, *gracias*," Claire said. "*Dispénseme.* Sorry to wake you. *Buenas noches. Adiós.*"

Claire snapped Alicia's phone shut.

"I knew Nina was a thief," Massie announced.

"Is that what she said?" Alicia asked. "Could you understand her?"

"She said *sí*, didn't she?" Massie said.

"She also said '*ladrona,*' which is *thief,*" Claire said. "I think."

"Then that proves it." Alicia nodded. "She stole their boots and everything else around here."

"Including my boyfriend," Claire mumbled.

"*Enough!*" Alicia and Massie shouted at Claire.

"Sorry," Claire said, even though she probably didn't mean it.

"We need to catch Nina in the act." Massie twirled her charm bracelet around her thin wrist.

"How are we going to do that?" Alicia whined.

"I know." Claire sat up tall in her seat. Her voice was confident and calm.

Isaac turned into the parking lot of the mall.

"Isaac, we can't stay."

"What?" Massie and Alicia snapped.

"The dance is in three days—we need clothes," Alicia said. "And we're already here."

"Since when do you tell Isaac what to do?" Massie added.

"Look, do you want to catch Nina or not?"

Massie felt a warm tingle of affection trickle down her spine. She couldn't believe Claire was being so bossy. She loved it.

"Massie?" Alicia pleaded. "We *have* to shop."

Isaac pulled into a parking spot but kept the motor running while he waited for the final word. "Massie?" he asked.

She pressed the automatic door lock button over and over again while she thought. The contact clicking added to the tension in the car.

"Massie," Alicia snapped, "can we please stay?"

Click.

"No." Massie shook her head. "The shopping will have to wait."

Isaac backed out of the spot and headed for home.

"This plan better work, Kuh-laire," Alicia hissed. "Because the last one you came up with sucked." She folded her arms across her chest and slouched down in the leather seat.

"It'll work, right?" Massie pinched the side of Claire's arm. "Right?" She pinched a little harder.

Claire nodded.

"Good," Massie said. "Because a shopportunity is a terrible thing to waste, and you're running out of chances."

"It'll work," Claire promised.

"If I were you, I'd start praying, just in case," Alicia said.

"Believe me," Claire assured her, "I am."

"To the house, Isaac," Massie instructed. "And take the shortcut. We have a lot of work to do."

MASSIE BLOCK'S CURRENT STATE OF THE UNION BLOG	
IN	**OUT**
Operation Booty Call	Operation Toe Jam
Crime Stoppers	Dress shoppers
Busted	Cleavage

Massie led Claire and Alicia around to the side entrance near the kitchen. Across the yard, the workmen were loading up their trucks with lumber and tools, ready to pack it in for the day. Claire couldn't make out any specific details in the dark, but it looked like the house had walls and half a roof.

"They sure are building that guesthouse quickly." Alicia sounded impressed.

"It doesn't feel very quick when you're sleeping in a bathtub," Claire mumbled.

"Huh?"

Massie elbowed Claire in the ribs. "Nothing," they said at the same time.

"Whatever." Alicia shrugged. Then she lowered her voice to a whisper. "Are you sure Todd will be home?" she asked Claire while Massie unlocked the door.

"If I know Todd, he's circling Inez while she's cooking dinner, hoping she'll accidentally drop some scraps on the floor." Massie reached in her bag for her keys.

Alicia and Massie started giggling.

"I'll admit, sometimes Todd may act like a dog but—," Claire started saying, but Massie cut her off.

"Look, Kuh-laire, if what you told us in the car about his spying is true, he's more like a weasel!" The door clicked open.

They walked into the warm kitchen and Claire knew right away that they were having Inez's crispy roast chicken. The rich, succulent smell of the browning skin was unmistakable. Claire peeked inside the pots on the stove and saw bacon mashed potatoes and noodle soup. At least dinner would be a success.

"Kendra." Judi followed Mrs. Block into the kitchen. "With all due respect, you can't just expect a child to want to show up to school on time. You have to teach them good habits by setting a good example and getting involved." They must have been in the kitchen having tea, because they dropped their empty cups in the sink.

"Well, Judi, with all due respect . . ." Kendra rested one hand on the kitchen counter and the other on her tiny waist. "This whole thing is new to me. You see, Massie never had a detention until today. In fact, she never got into any trouble at all until she started hanging out with—"

"Hi, Mom."

Kendra and Judi whipped their heads around and gasped when they saw the girls standing there.

"Uh, hi, sweetie, how was school?" Kendra asked.

"Fine," Massie said. "Where's Todd?"

"Upstairs, practicing his tuba." Judi gave Claire a We-need-to-talk-about-those-detentions look. Claire rolled her eyes.

Inez hurried into the kitchen, frantically waving her arms like she was trying to clear a cloud of smoke. "What are you doing in my kitchen before dinner?" She clapped her hands three times. "Get out! Out!"

Everyone left without saying a word.

Massie led Claire and Alicia upstairs to Todd's room. She reached the top and turned around. "Why are our mothers fighting about discipline?" She said "discipline" like she would say "dog poo."

"I dunno. But it's weird. It sounded like your mother was about to blame me for the detentions."

"I wouldn't be surprised," Alicia huffed as she climbed the last stair. "She used to blame me every time Massie got a wrong answer on a test."

"Better you than me." Massie winked, then turned toward Todd's room.

Once they were outside his door, Claire squeezed her way past Massie and gently placed her hand on the brass knob. She could hear the farting sound of Todd's tuba through the walls. "Allow me," she whispered. And to her surprise, Massie and Alicia willingly agreed.

Claire counted to three inside her head and then pushed open the door. "Hi-ya!" she shouted and kicked her leg like a kung fu expert when she entered his room.

Massie and Alicia screamed, "Hi-ya!" too, then sliced the air with the sides of their palms. Even though she was supposed to act mean and angry, Claire couldn't help smiling at their improvised entrance.

Todd lifted half of his mouth off the tuba. "Hello, angels. Does this make me Charlie?"

"Where's your spy gear?" Claire asked.

"What spy gear?" Todd widened his eyes, trying to look innocent.

"Massie, you search under the bed. Alicia, you check the drawers. I'll take the closet."

"What are you doing?" Todd jumped to his feet. "Help, police!" He started blowing his tuba like a car alarm. *Puurp . . . puurp . . . puurp . . .* "Police! I'm being robbed!" *Puurp . . . puurp . . . puurp . . .*

"We should be the ones calling the police." Claire pulled Todd's clothes out of his closet and threw them on the floor. "It's illegal to spy on people."

"Not in New York State," Todd said. "Hidden cameras are legal here as long as one party knows about it. And I'm that party." He handed Claire the legal document that had come with his camera equipment. "See?"

Claire pretended to read it, but she was angry and couldn't focus. She threw the document on the floor. "Well I don't think mom and dad will care if it's legal or not, especially since you've already been grounded for eavesdropping." She tapped her stubby fingernails against his closet door. They had been chewed so much, it actually hurt. "I wouldn't be surprised if mom grounded you from playing in the finals game."

Massie and Alicia folded their arms across their chests like threatening bodyguards.

"Okay, fine. It's in the box marked Dirty Old Underwear."

Claire searched the floor of his closet.

"Up top." Todd pointed to the shelf above his hanging clothes.

Claire jumped up and knocked the Adidas shoe box to the floor. It fell to the floor and spilled open.

"Ew!" Claire shrieked. "There's nothing in here but dirty old underwear. What's wrong with you?"

"Oops, wrong box." Todd grinned. "I keep those for good luck."

"Well, you're gonna need 'em if you don't tell us where the spy gear is," Massie said.

"Try the box that says Operation Underpants," he offered.

"What is with your family and operations?" Alicia asked.

Claire shrugged as she knocked the L. L. Bean shoe box off the shelf.

"Easy." Todd threw his tuba on the bed and rushed over to the closet. "This stuff is fragile."

Claire gave a dramatic sigh before lifting the lid. "Ready?" She loved that she was in control of the situation, and was trying to milk it as much as she could.

"Yeah," Massie insisted. "Open it already."

"Hurry," Alicia said.

"Here goes." Claire lifted the lid. A swatch of red velvet material lined the inside of the box.

"Hey, that's my Christmas scarf!" Massie shrieked. "Where did you get that?"

"It was a gift from Nina. Because she thought I was cute."

"Well, it's mine." Massie tugged on the red velvet, knocking around the little camera that had been resting on top of it.

Alicia reached into the shoe box and pulled out something that looked like a black button. "What is this?" she asked.

"It's a button cam," Todd explained.

"Cam," Claire sighed, then turned to Massie.

"Oh no," Massie said. "Don't start thinking about him now."

"Todd said it, I didn't. It's just that I have no idea what we could have possibly done wrong—"

"Not now." Massie turned to face Todd. "So how does this work?"

Todd folded his arms, then turned his back on the girls.

"Todd, you better talk or else no soccer game." Claire was amazed at how much she was able to sound like her mother when she wanted to. "And without that, you have absolutely no chance of ever getting a girl to like you."

"Fine."

Todd explained how to work the hidden camera and showed the girls how to watch the feed on a TV. Once they understood how to hook everything up, Alicia took the camera and dropped it in her signature brown-and-black Fendi change purse.

"Alicia, are you sure you'll be able to plant it on Nina without her knowing?" Massie asked.

"Given," Alicia said with a big, toothy smile.

"Okay, then tomorrow after school we'll meet in the DJ booth to watch the footage," Massie said, reviewing the plan. "Todd, if you ever tell anyone about this, I'll tell every girl at OCD that you talk to your fingers."

Todd whimpered and shook his head.

"Then not a word to anyone." Massie narrowed her eyes. "Not even Mr. Thumb."

Alicia and Claire giggled. Todd threw a sneaker at them on their way out, but Massie shut the door before they got hit. "I'm so not done with you yet, Lyons," Massie shouted through the door. "*So not!*"

"Now remember," Massie whispered before Alicia left the estate, "not a word of this to Kristen and Dylan. For some sick reason, they seem to like Nina, and they may end up telling her." She held out her pinky.

Alicia wrapped her finger around Massie's and swore. Then Claire did the same.

The next afternoon, Claire could hardly sit still through her classes. She couldn't wait to see what Nina was really like. If her plan worked, Massie and Alicia would be forever grateful. And if it didn't, they'd never listen to her ideas again. The second the bell rang; Claire bolted out of English and ran down the hall.

When she got to the booth, Alicia and Massie were already there, staring at the tiny TV monitor they'd gotten from Todd.

"This is so strange," Massie noted. "The camera's not moving."

Claire pushed her way closer to the monitor. They were looking at a lopsided shot of a gray cement floor and the legs of a bench. A white sweat sock was lying in the background. "Maybe she fainted."

"I wish," Alicia murmured.

"Did one of you tell Kristen or Dylan?" Massie looked directly at Claire with her amber eyes. It felt like they were shooting heat rays straight to the back of her skull.

"I didn't," Alicia promised.

"Me either," Claire added. "Maybe it fell off."

"How could it? I stuck it to the outside of her bag."

"Duh." Massie rolled her eyes. "She's a notorious bag-swinger. I noticed that the first day I met her. I assumed you would have picked up on it too."

Alicia shrugged. She looked down and aimlessly began drawing tight spirals on a wooden desk with her silver Tiffany pen.

"This sucks," Massie stated matter-of-factly.

"I knew we should have gone shopping." Alicia slammed her pen down. "At least we would have had outfits for the dance."

Claire was desperate to lighten the mood. "Hey, wouldn't it be weird if we saw our own backs on the camera and then we turned around and Nina was standing right behind us?"

Suddenly the girls heard someone sniffle behind them. All three of them screamed and jumped to their feet. They started waving their arms and hopping up and down in hysterics.

"What is your problem?" Kristen was standing in the doorway with tears rolling down her cheeks.

"Ehmagod Kristen." Massie put her hand on her heart. "You scared us."

"Who did you think it was?" Kristen asked. "Chucky?"

The girls started laughing. Kristen waited patiently for them to stop.

"How did you find us?" Massie asked.

"I saw Claire run here after class and I—," Kristen said. "Wait—do you not want me here?"

"No, it's not that," Alicia explained. "We just thought you had soccer practice."

"That's Tuesdays and Thursdays," Kristen corrected. "Where's Dylan?"

"She went home early because she's sick," Massie reminded her. "You know that."

"Oh yeah." Kristen looked at the ground. She twirled her index finger around her blond hair while a stream of tears fell down her cheeks.

"What's wrong?" Claire finally asked.

She burst into hysterical sobs. "My mom is insisting on chaperoning the dance because I've been getting so many detentions lately."

"What?" Massie screeched.

"No offense, but that woman needs to join a gym or something," Alicia offered. "She's obsessed with everything you do."

"That *woman* is her *mother*," Claire said. "Don't you guys ever get in trouble?"

Alicia and Massie looked at each other and shook their heads.

"How am I ever going to kiss Kemp Hurley if my mom is watching me all night?" Kristen whined. "I'll never win that bet, unless . . ." Her voice trailed off.

"Unless what?" Massie asked.

"Unless Dylan's flu gets worse." Kristen closed her eyes, crossed her fingers, and bit her bottom lip. She looked like an *American Idol* contestant waiting to hear if she'd won.

Claire was reminded of the dance and sighed. "Can we go to the mall?" she asked.

Massie whipped her head around. "*Kuh-laire*, did you just say what I think you said?"

"Seriously," Alicia said. "That's my line."

"I know, but maybe if I have a cute outfit, Cam will change his mind."

"I like the way you're thinking," Alicia purred.

"I think you should buy a cute outfit, but not for Cam," Massie suggested. "You need to move on. We all do. Maybe you should kiss someone else at the dance."

"I could never—"

"She's not going to be part of the bet now, is she?" Kristen asked. "I mean, no offense, Claire, but I really want those boots."

"I told you, I don't want to kiss someone as part of a bet," Claire reminded her.

"I think you should do it to teach Cam a lesson." Massie's lips curled up in a devilish way.

"Are you going to do that to Derrington?" Claire asked.

"Thinking about it." Massie took out her Cinnabon lip gloss and patted it on her lips with the wand. Then she puckered up and blew an air kiss. "Maybe you should ask the hearts who you're going to kiss."

"Good idea." Claire reached into her coat pocket and pried the plastic bag open with her fingers. Her supply was running short, and it took a few seconds for her to find a heart that hadn't been crushed. There was one left. "Okay." She sighed. "Heart, when I open my eyes after my first kiss, will it be Cam Fisher I'm looking at?

Claire pulled the blue heart out of her pocket and flipped it over. She felt herself smile before she read it aloud.

"What does it say?" Massie asked.

"Read it," Alicia urged.

"Come on," Kristen said.

Claire took a deep breath. **"Whatever Your Heart Desires."**

The girls jumped up and down and clapped for Claire's good fortune, while she sucked on the heart, trying as hard as she could not to let it break.

The girls were sitting at number eighteen, their usual lunch table in the Café. Alicia was licking the tops of her California rolls, Claire was eating a bowl of Cap'n Crunch, Kristen was drinking whole milk from the carton, and Dylan was pulling the cheese off her pizza, hoping to lose a few extra pounds before the big dance. Massie was the only one without an appetite. How could she possibly digest anything when all the girls in school looked like they were about to audition for a Christina Aguilera video?

Massie made an I-just-sucked-a-lemon face. "Why does everyone look so Nina-ish today?"

"I can't believe how many people are copying her. How ticepath." Kristen sat up in her chair so she could pull her denim miniskirt out of her butt.

"I doh, id is pathetic." Dylan coughed and pulled a tin of imported French lemon drops out of the side pocket on her Chinese silk bathrobe. She was wearing it over jeans, and it actually looked kind of fashion-forward, even though she was just being sick and lazy.

Massie was tempted to call them hypocrites but decided against it. She didn't want to push Kristen and Dylan any closer to Nina than they already were.

"Massie, how are you going to wear your hair tomorrow night?" Alicia asked as she took a sip of her virgin cosmopolitan. Suddenly, she stuck out her pink tongue. "Ew, this tastes like warm Kool-Aid."

"Oooh, that reminds me. . . ." Massie pulled out her cell phone and speed dialed Jakkob. "I need to schedule an updo." She picked at the whole-wheat toast crust on her tuna sandwich while she waited for someone at the salon to answer. "Yes, hi, Casey, this is Massie Block. . . . Bean is great, thanks. She loves the styling gel you gave her. . . . Listen, I was wondering if I could borrow Jakkob tomorrow at around four-ish for a quick updo. I have a big event tomorrow night and I have to look ah-mazing." She winked at Claire when she said that. "Four-fifteen? Perfect . . . see you then." She chucked her tuna on wheat in the trash and folded her arms across her chest. "Done."

"I heard your bommy is coming to the dance." Dylan turned to Kristen. She laced her fingers behind her head and leaned back in her chair. "That should bake for a romantic evening with Kemp Hurley."

"Oh, like Chris Plovert is going to think your sinusitis is hot?" Kristen snapped back.

"Maybe you two should call off this bet," Massie suggested. "It's tearing you apart."

"Yeah. Besides, you should only kiss someone if you really love them. Not just to do it."

"Listen to the expert." Dylan smirked. "Cam won't even talk to you."

"Ouch," Alicia said.

"He'll come around." Claire nodded. "The hearts said so."

A few seconds later Massie got a text message. She wanted it to be Derrington so badly, she waited a few seconds before she checked it. It was always better be to full of hope than disappointment.

When she finally looked, her heart sank. It was from Claire.

CLAIRE: Has Derrington called U yet?
MASSIE: ☹
CLAIRE: Cam hasn't called either. I should call. The kiss is tomorrow.

"Don't call him, Kuh-laire. Make him come to you."

Claire shot Massie a Thanks-a-lot-for-betraying-my-confidence look, but Massie didn't care. There was only so much Dr. Phil she could give, especially when things were so terrible with Derrington. She had gone through two tubes of Glossip Girl in one week, and the flavors had been Raisin Pudding and Hay. The stress was driving her to overapply.

"That's what Deena always says. Bake them cub to you."

"I love that you're finally starting to take Nina's advice," Kristen said. "If there's one thing she knows about, it's boys."

"I like to think I know a little more than just that," Nina purred as she dropped a chair down at number eighteen and sat. She was wearing one of Sage's Virgins for Life T-shirts, with the word *NOT* written across it in red paint.

"FYI, I wasn't taking *her* advice," Massie corrected. "I just read about male psychology in *Teen Vogue*."

"It's okay to admit you want to be like me. Everyone else has." Nina looked around the Café and smiled at all of the girls who were wobbling around in knee-high boots, microminis, and tight, revealing tops. "Look, Kristen." Nina was pointing to a group of girls wearing cowboy hats. "I told you the hat thing would catch on."

"Ehmagod." Kristen smiled brightly. "You were so right."

"I wonder what I am better at?" Nina asked no one in particular. "Fashion advice or guy advice?"

"Nina, are you a magician?" Massie asked.

"No . . ."

"Then why are you acting all delusional?"

"Uh, Massie," Kristen whispered softly, "magicians do *illusions*, not *de*-lusions."

Massie felt the prickly heat of embarrassment tickle her spine. "It's not like she'll know the difference. She's from Spain."

"Who are you calling a magician?" Nina asked as a group of giddy girls approached their table and hovered around her.

"Nina, you have to help me." Cookie Holsen reached into her purple Dooney & Bourke Nile duffel and pulled out two different outfits. One was a red BCBG satin dress with Spanish ruffles around the sleeves and the other was a black see-through V-necked tank top and a pair of leather short shorts.

Nina rubbed each outfit between her thumbs and sighed. "Do you have to ask?"

"The leather short shorts?" Cookie offered.

"Given!"

"Hey, that's my word," Alicia whispered to Massie.

"Not anymore," Massie whispered back. "She steals everything."

"Cookie." Massie curled her index finger so the girl would lean toward her. Once their eyes met, Massie whispered, "If you want to look *stylish*, I suggest the red dress. Ruffles are very hot right now."

"I want to look like Nina," Cookie said. "Besides, she has way more experience with boys, so I kinda want to take her advice for now. No offense." The two girls standing behind her nodded their heads in agreement, then revealed bags full of outfits that were ready for Nina's approval.

"You know, Massie," said Elise West, one of Cookie's friends, "you should have Nina contribute to your blog. You know, when it comes to fashion and boys. Oh, and makeup."

"Or maybe she should write the whole thing," offered Alexis Higgins, Cookie's other friend.

"She's right, Nina." Cookie was shifting nervously from one high-heeled boot to the other. "You have better advice than anyone else in the entire school."

Massie could have sworn Cookie was looking right at her when she said that. And she could feel her insides starting to tremble. It was a combination of extreme anger and pain. Nina was destroying her empire. And she wasn't even famous!

Nina must have sensed Massie's frustration. "What is that expression you Americans use?" She snapped her fingers a few times as if that would somehow help her remember. "Ah, yes. Don't be sad over milk?"

"You mean, no use crying over spilt milk?" Cookie shouted.

"Yes, that's it." Nina smiled. "Massie, there's no use crying over spilt milk. There's a new fashion goddess in town, and you have to get over it."

"You're right." Massie half-smiled. She could feel her friends' eyes on her.

"She is?" Alicia asked.

"Yup." Massie grabbed the milk carton away from Kristen's thirsty lips and in one swift motion dumped the contents on Nina. "There's no use crying over spilt milk." It drenched her Virgins for Life shirt and soaked the ends of Cookie's tangled black hair.

Everyone broke into a fit of laughter except Nina, Cookie, and her two friends. It was like they had been frozen solid with their mouths open.

Suddenly, a bony hand clamped down on Massie's shoulder. A long, brittle fingernail dug into the back of her neck, and she wondered if a bird might have flown in through the window and landed on her. She turned her head slowly, just in case she was right.

"*Detention!*" Principal Burns squawked. She handed Massie a pink slip. "That makes three in one week, Miss Block."

Massie opened her mouth to respond, but Principal Burns cut her off before she could manage to get out the first syllable.

"One more and you'll be suspended." She circled Massie's chair, never taking her beady black eyes off Massie's face.

Nina was leaning back in her chair wearing a cocky smile.

Principal Burns finally turned her attention to Alicia.

"What did I do?" Alicia's brown eyes were wide with innocence.

"You didn't do anything. I came to give you this breaking news report." Principal Burns handed Alicia a white paper napkin covered in her ultra-tiny, all-caps handwriting. There was a small coffee stain in the lower left-hand corner. "Apparently, a miniature camera was found in the boys' locker room at Briarwood. Coach Pierce is accusing Grayson Academy of espionage. He's pressuring the athletics board to cancel the finals game until there has been a full investigation."

Massie felt her heartbeat quicken.

"No!" Kristen shouted. "He can't call off the finals. I've been waiting all year for this game."

"Well, you may want to consider a class in time management, Miss Gregory," Principal Burns said. "Now I suggest you hurry, Alicia. The public deserves to know what's going on here."

"I'm on it." Alicia saluted the principal, then turned and walked away.

"I said hurry!" Principal Burns shouted.

"I am!" Alicia said.

Massie was so excited by the news, she could hardly sit still. As soon as Principal Burns left, she pulled out her cell phone and sent an urgent message to Claire and Alicia.

MASSIE: Meet me on the library steps after detention. Wear dark clothes. Come alone. We're going in.

MASSIE BLOCK'S CURRENT STATE OF THE UNION BLOG	
IN	**OUT**
Short hair	Short shorts
Milk	Cookies
Spy cam	Claire's Cam

Claire, Massie, and Alicia were lying flat on their bellies with their arms around each other's backs. It was all they could do to keep from freezing on the icy cold pavement beneath them. They were on the ground below the last row of bleachers in Briarwood's soccer stadium, safely hidden from view while they waited patiently for the right time to make their move.

"Look," Claire said when she saw Cam. He shuffled out of the locker room and onto the field. "He got a new gym bag." He threw the brown-and-white Puma duffel over his shoulder and zipped up his worn leather jacket.

"Spying is awesome." Massie paused for a second before continuing. "Except for what Todd did—that was pervy times ten."

"This is a whole new way to get gossip," suggested Alicia

"It sucks," Claire groaned. "It's just another bitter reminder of how much I miss Cam." He waited by the goalie net for Derrington and Chris Plovert to catch up. It was obvious they were tired, because they had the posture of guys who'd lost the big game, not practiced for it. For a second, Claire caught herself feeling sorry for Cam and wished that she could bring him a Coke or a bag of Hot Cheetos. But then she remembered how he'd run away from her less than a week ago and decided that if anyone should be doling out the "feel better" gifts, it should be him.

Claire checked Massie's face for signs of Derrington grief, but her expression gave away nothing. Her stare was hard and emotionless; it was the same expression she'd worn when Principal Burns was lecturing her about throwing milk at Nina.

When the boys disappeared into the distance, Massie sighed. "That's the last of them." She used purple nail polish to cross their three names off the team list Todd had slipped them after school. "The locker room should be empty now."

"Do you think they miss us?" Claire buried her face in her hands as soon as the words came out of her mouth, as if she were protecting herself from an inevitable slap.

"Kuh-laire!" Alicia and Massie shouted.

"Are you a midget?" Massie asked.

"No."

"Then get over him!"

Alicia laughed, then high-fived Massie.

"Can you?" Claire asked. "Are you honestly over Derrington?" Then she turned to Alicia. "And are you over the fact that Josh is going to the dance with someone else, namely your cousin? Because if you are, tell me how you did it."

Claire felt the tears coming. She was so upset with

herself for getting emotional; she sat up and punched herself in the thigh.

Massie grabbed Claire's fist. "What difference does it
make if I'm over Derrington or not?" she said in a soft,
soothing voice. "The point is, I have to act like I am. If I
didn't, I'd be a mess, like you."

"I don't want to be a mess anymore," Claire sniffled. But
she couldn't help herself. It was like picking a scab. She
was incapable of letting herself heal.

"Let's do this." Alicia lifted the hood on her black cashmere sweater and covered her head. "Let's catch the girl
who's responsible for our grief. It's the only way we'll ever
recover."

"She's right," Massie agreed.

"Okay." Claire took a deep breath and forced herself to
smile.

"How much do we love your Nurse Adele connection?"
Massie covered her face with a black pashmina. "Why didn't
I ever think of becoming friends with the nurse? After all,
she *is* the keeper of the lost and found. I should have seen
the potential in that way before Claire did."

"Like you would ever wear lost clothes," Alicia said.

"True." Massie sniffed the black pashmina and winced.
"This smells like grandmother."

"Well, I actually *like* Nurse Adele." Claire slipped on a
black ski cap and tucked her white-blond hair inside.

"You just like her because she lets you take whatever
you want from her office," Alicia added.

"That's not true!" Claire snapped. "She was my first friend at OCD."

"Ew, she's the nurse." Alicia rolled her eyes.

"So?"

"Focus." Massie clapped her hands and lifted a doctor's mask over her face. Claire and Alicia did the same. Massie started humming the theme song to *Mission Impossible* as the girls made their way down from the bleachers to the field. It wasn't long before Claire and Alicia started singing along. When they reached the outside of the locker room, they pressed their backs up against the yellow brick walls, like cops on the verge of busting into a drug dealer's apartment.

"Okay, so what exactly are we looking for?" Claire whispered.

"I dunno," Massie said. "Proof that Nina is stealing, I guess."

"Just because her camera was here doesn't mean we're going to find any clues," Alicia said.

"I know, but it's the only lead we have," Massie snapped. "Come on." She pressed her shoulder into the blue door outside the locker room and pushed it open quietly.

"Ew." Alicia fanned the air the second they stepped inside.

"It smells like sweat and duct tape." Massie winced. "And jockstraps."

Claire covered her nose with the collar of her black windbreaker.

"How do you know what jockstraps smell like?" Alicia giggled.

"I heard Nina describe it in her sleep," Massie said.

Alicia cracked up. Claire meant to laugh, but she was too busy examining the rows of green lockers, wondering which one belonged to Cam.

The sound of dripping water echoed from the showers.

Plip. Plip. Plip.

"Hullo," Massie called. "Anyone in here?"

No one answered back.

"Look," Alicia whispered. She was pointing at a locker with a bright pink lock.

"What kind of guy would have a pink lock?" Claire asked.

"Eli." Massie giggled.

"Yeah, but he never made the team," Claire reminded her.

They walked closer.

"It kinda looks like Kristen's."

"Try her combo," Claire suggested. "It's Beckham's birthday, 0502."

"She's right!"

Massie looked around for possible intruders one last time, and then she grabbed the lock. She turned the dial right, left, all the way around to the right, and then a quick left. She took a deep breath and tugged. The lock snapped open.

The girls gasped.

Massie put the lock in her pocket, then lifted the metal hinge. "We're in," she said. She pulled back the squeaky green door and immediately covered her nose. The spicy smell of men's cologne was everywhere.

"That's Polo," Alicia said. She pushed Massie and Claire out of the way and practically stepped inside the locker. After a few deep inhales, Alicia ran her fingers over the blue blazer that was hanging on the back hook, took one more sniff, and then declared, "This locker belongs to Josh Hotz."

"How do you know?" Claire asked.

"Polo cologne, Ralph Lauren blazer, and these." She opened the door as wide as it would go and pointed to the newspaper clippings that were taped to the inside. "These are the articles about him getting expelled from Hotchkiss for pulling the fire alarm." Alicia lifted Josh's blazer off the hook and tried it on. She lifted the sleeves to her nose and inhaled deeply.

"Mmmmm." She made the same noise that Dylan made whenever she smelled a fresh batch of blueberry muffins in the Café. "Ralph, how *do* you do it?"

Claire and Massie pushed Alicia aside and took a closer look.

"Gross." Massie lifted a dirty sweat sock off the bottom of the locker. "All the guys from the Tomahawks signed this to welcome him to the team," Massie said.

Claire secretly looked for Cam's signature. She felt her

palms itch the instant she saw his slanted handwriting: *Hotchkiss sucks! Welcome to Briarwood.*

"Why would Josh steal Kristen's bike lock?" Alicia asked.

"He wouldn't." Claire pulled a piece of white monogrammed stationery off the top shelf. It said ALICIA RIVERA in silver block letters.

"That's my personalized stationery," Alicia gasped. "How did he get that?"

Claire cleared her throat and read the letter out loud.

Dear Josh,

I put a secret Spanish victory spell on this lock. Use it one week before the game and the Tummyhocks will win the finals. But if you tell anyone where you got it or why you're using it, the spell will turn into a curse. You will lose the game and break an ankle.

Love,

Nina

"Ew, look!" Claire cried out. "She kissed the page with her red lipstick."

"Alicia, is there such a thing as a Spanish victory spell?" Massie asked.

"Not that I know of."

"Then why would she want Josh to have—?"

"Because of that." Claire pointed to a gray Kenneth Cole shoe bag that was taped to the top shelf of Josh's locker. She stretched her arms above her head. "I can't reach it."

Massie grabbed the end of one of the wooden benches. "Alicia, give me a hand."

Alicia touched the other side of the bench while Massie tried her hardest to lift it.

"Grab it," Massie grunted.

"I am," Alicia whined.

Eventually Massie managed to slide the bench across the floor on her own. It was the first time Claire had ever seen her do anything remotely physical, and she couldn't help giggling.

Once the bench was in place, Claire stepped up and pulled the Kenneth Cole bag down with little effort.

"Hey! That's my shoe bag."

"How do you know?" Massie asked. "Everyone in Westchester shops at Kenneth Cole."

"Check out the bottom," Alicia offered.

Claire lifted the bag, and sure enough, it read, "AR & RL" in gold metallic ink.

"Who is RL?" Claire asked

"Ralph Lauren." Massie rolled her eyes.

Alicia giggled. "I didn't want Ralph to be upset that I bought Kenneth Cole, so I gave him a little secret reassurance."

"No comment." Massie smirked.

"Ready?" Claire shook the bag. She opened it slowly. The girls were so anxious to see what was inside, they leaned closer and bumped heads.

"Give it to me." Massie pulled the bag away from Claire and dumped everything onto the floor.

"No." Alicia paused. "Way."

"Wow," Claire gasped

"Ehmagod," Massie whispered.

Everyone's stolen loot was lying on the cold gray floor of the boys' locker room. Alicia's argyle socks, Massie's hair crimper, Natalie Nussbaum's Chococat pencil case, Mrs. Beeline's red Montblanc pen, Jessi Rowan's Kipling monkey key chain, and at least a dozen tubes and jars of makeup.

"Hey, that's the eyeliner Eli bought at the MAC counter," Alicia said.

"How do you know it's his?" Claire asked.

"Because no girl I know would ever buy hot pink eyeliner called Tender. I remember seeing him try it on when I bumped into him at the mall. Nina was with me."

"Nina must have given Josh the lock so she would have a secret place to hide her stash."

"How could he not know it was there?" Claire asked.

"Boys are idiots," Alicia said with a nod.

"I agree." Claire looked down at her high-tops.

"She is so dead." Alicia tried to crack her knuckles.

"*Adiós, muchacha.*" Massie grinned evilly.

"*Hasta la vista*, baby," Claire added.

"*Ciao, bella*," Alicia said.

"Isn't that Italian?" Massie asked.

"I dunno." Alicia shrugged. "It still means 'She's so dead,' right?"

"*Sí,*" Massie said.

"*Sí* her later." Claire gave a great big smile.

They dropped the stolen items back in the shoe bag and Massie stuffed it under her coat. Once everything was back in Josh's locker, they headed toward the parking lot to meet Isaac.

"When are we going to bust her?" Claire asked. "Can we do it tonight?"

"Tonight? I'm not ready for a bust," Alicia said. "I have math homework."

"Then when?" Claire heard herself whine.

"Relax. We have to lie in the weeds and think about this for a minute. We can't just pounce. We need to wait a couple of weeks." Isaac flashed his headlights. Massie waved.

"I can't wait that long. She stole more than a stupid pair of socks from me. She took Cam. I say we get her at the dance tomorrow night."

The girls stopped walking and Claire instantly regretted trying to boss them around. Massie's amber eyes flickered back and forth while she thought, and Claire bit her thumbnail and waited for Massie to respond.

"Done," Massie said.

Claire sighed.

"Done," Alicia said.

"And done," Claire said. "We're not going to the dance solo. We have a date with revenge."

"What does one wear on a date with revenge?" Alicia asked.

"A big fat smile," Massie offered.

"In that case," Claire said, "I'm already dressed."

Massie could smell the flower and plant essences in her freshly coiffed hair as she slipped off her white cashmere coat. Jakkob had given her a half-down, half-up hairdo and fastened the shorter layers with glittery rhinestone barrettes. These complimented the fifteen brooches she had attached to her white wool tea-length sleeveless Prada dress. She felt like a beautiful snow angel, even though she didn't have a date.

"Jackie, would you mind putting these garment bags with my coat?" Massie handed the coat check girl a heap of clothes. Jackie almost fell over when she grabbed them but somehow managed to steady herself long enough to hang them on one of the silver racks behind her long desk.

"What's in there?" Claire asked as she unzipped her ski jacket.

"I brought an outfit for Kristen and a few different options for us in case we changed our minds when we got here." Massie took a minute to study Claire's outfit now that they were standing under the red party lights. "I should have given you one of my formal coats. That thing should not be allowed out past five."

"I love my ski jacket." Claire handed it to Jackie.

205

"I love my dad, but I don't bring him to dances," Massie countered.

"Well, what do you think of my dress?" Claire spun. Her ice blue chiffon Bebe dress floated above her knees as she twirled. "Think it'll make Cam want to kiss me?"

Massie slapped Claire on the shoulder. "Don't do that here."

Claire lost her balance and had to grab onto the corner of Jackie's coat check desk to keep from falling. "Ouch! What was that for?"

"You have to act confident," Massie whispered. "From this moment on, act like you ah-dore your outfit. People can smell insecurity, and it's a major turnoff."

"But I really do like my outfit. It's Cam I'm—"

Massie held her freshly moisturized palm in front of Claire's face. "Enough. There are a hundred other guys at this dance who will love your dress." Truth be told, Claire's outfit was a little too sweet for Massie's taste, but it suited Claire.

Jackie handed the girls coat check tags and stickers that said, I LOVE YOU. MY NAME IS_____. Claire wrote her name in the space, peeled off the back, and stuck it to her dress.

Massie crumpled hers up and left it on the desk. "Let's go," she said.

"Why don't you want your sticker?" Claire asked.

"The glue is terrible on wool."

The muffled sound of Ashlee Simpson's "La La" seeped through the walls of the gym and flooded the hallway. The closer they got to the doors, the more cheering and laughing they heard.

"You okay?" Claire asked Massie before they walked inside.

"Yeah, why?"

"You're holding your belly." Claire looked concerned.

"Oh." Massie dropped her hand. "It's nothing. I'm fine," she said, even though she could feel her stomach in her throat. She always felt like that just before making an entrance. And tonight she actually had real reasons to feel nervous. *What if I see Derrington? What if I don't? Will he like what I did with my brooches? Will anyone ask me to dance? What if the Nina revenge plan doesn't work?* Massie casually lifted her arms to let her pits air out before she walked inside.

They were greeted at the gym's entrance by a handsome man dressed in a tuxedo. He looked like a Calvin Klein model. "Welcome, ladies, you look beautiful tonight. Happy Valentine's Day." He held the doors open for them. "Enjoy the dance."

"We'll try," Claire sighed.

Massie elbowed her in the ribs. "Confidence," she whispered again.

"Sorry."

"Ehmagod," was all Massie could say when she saw the inside of the gym. It had been completely transformed.

All of the fluorescent lightbulbs had been removed and replaced with pink ones, giving the room a warm, rosy glow.

Long black lace ribbons dotted with cinnamon hearts dangled from the ceiling and hovered a few inches above the floor. Everyone was pushing them aside as they walked. They reminded Massie of those long rubber strips that cleaned the Range Rover at the car wash. Four tall silver machines, one in each corner of the room, blew big red bubbles that drifted across the entire gym. The DJ booth was covered in red shag carpet and glitter. The DJ wore only a diaper, like Cupid. It looked like everyone in the entire county was there. The room was packed.

"Look." Claire hit Massie on the arm, then pointed to the giant heart-shaped ice sculpture in the middle of the gym.

Cam and Chris Plovert were laughing hysterically because Derrington had licked the ice and was pretending to be stuck.

Massie was starting to sweat all over again. How could the boys be having so much fun without her? She wanted to run to the bathroom, regloss, wipe her pits, and check her hair, but she had to follow her own advice and act confident. "Children." She shook her head.

"This is stupid," Claire said. "Shouldn't we say hi or something?"

"No, let's go find everyone," Massie instructed.

Claire stomped her foot. "How am I going to kiss him if I can't even talk to him?"

"You're not. Look, there's Kristen and her mom. Let's mingle. We don't want to be seen standing by the door watching the party—it makes us look like pathetic losers."

Massie pulled Claire over to the round table where the Gregorys were nibbling on red-frosted sugar cookies. She rolled her shoulders back and lifted her head as she walked, just in case Derrington happened to notice her.

"Hey." Kristen jumped out of her seat and hugged Massie. She was wearing thick gray pleated slacks and a white turtleneck sweater with a blue teddy bear hugging a heart knit right into the front. The heart said, "I'm Blue Without You," in pink script.

"Thank Gawd you're finally here," Kristen whispered in Massie's ear as she adjusted her navy beret. "You have to get me away from her. Look what she made me wear. There's no *way* I can talk to Kemp in this."

Massie gave her a reassuring squeeze before pulling away. In the distance, Strawberry was dancing like a maniac to a Simple Plan song, until she slipped on a soapy bubble and fell.

"I think I just willed that to happen."

Claire and Kristen laughed.

"That's what you get for telling on us," Massie said to no one in particular.

"It's not funny. She could be hurt." Mrs. Gregory ran over to Strawberry, who was rolling around on the floor, grabbing her kneecap.

"Thank Gawd she's finally gone." Kristen held out her hand and Massie gave her the coat check ticket.

"Isn't your mother going to notice you're in a different outfit?" Claire asked.

"Hopefully I can change, kiss Kemp Hurley, win the bet, and change back before she notices," Kristen said. "Has anyone seen Landy?"

"Dylan couldn't come," Massie told them. "Her mother said she was too sick."

"Awesome! Does this mean I automatically win the bet? Where's Nina?"

"I don't think so," Claire said.

"Why?" Kristen stomped her foot.

"Because Dylan's sitting over there with Chris Plovert." Claire pointed to the buffet. "Look, she's smearing icing on his cast."

"No yaw." Kristen looked stunned. "She's way too sick to be out."

"I think she looks good," Claire put in.

Massie agreed. Dylan's red ringlets were perfectly conditioned so that they bounced and gleamed every time she moved her head. She was wearing a slimming Louis Vuitton black V-necked dress with a tulle tutu attached to the bottom. It was elegant and tasteful and probably stolen from her mother's closet.

As if she could read Massie's mind, Dylan looked up and waved them over.

"What are you doing here?" Kristen asked. "I thought your mother wanted you to stay in bed."

"Doesn't bean I'm going do." She was obviously trying to sound cool in front of Chris.

"Ye-ah, I love it." Chris tossed his thick silver tie over his shoulder and high-fived her.

Dylan looked at Kristen and smirked.

"I like your dress," Claire said.

"I sure could have used a pair of cool boots to wear with it though." She turned to Kristen. "But I should have those any minute now."

Kristen's cheeks turned dark red. "Hey, Chris, have you seen Kemp?" She smeared a coat of gloss across her thin lips.

"I think he went to flirt with the cute coat check girl," Chris said as he slid a fork inside his cast and scratched his leg. "Wait." He stopped scratching. "Aren't you his date?"

"No." Kristen turned to leave. "He's mine." She flicked the coat check ticket with her index finger and took off.

"Dice sweater." Dylan chuckled as she watched Kristen stomp across the gym, pushing bubbles out of her way with every angry step she took.

The music suddenly got louder, and Massie and Claire turned their backs on Dylan and Chris to look at the dance floor. Suddenly the party was in full swing.

The DJ had a mic but shouted anyway. "I need a lot of cooooool couples on the dance floor because it's getting 'Hot in Herre,'" he said before blasting Nelly's old hit. Suddenly Massie felt like she didn't belong. The dance floor was packed with couples.

Massie felt her phone vibrating and was instantly

relieved. She was tired of looking at happy people. She snapped open her silver-and-black snakeskin Isabella Fiore clutch and checked the display screen on her phone. Alicia had sent a text message. Massie retrieved it quickly so that anyone watching her would think she had important business to take care of. Way more important than dancing.

ALICIA: ? Are U?
MASSIE: Buffet table with C and D. U?
ALICIA: Just got here with Nina. She's already dancing. Look.

Massie scoped the dance floor like she was desperately looking for someone. If anyone was still watching her, hopefully they would conclude that the important caller needed Massie to find someone urgently.

"What's wrong?" Claire was bopping her head to the beat of the song.

Massie didn't say a word, so Claire followed her gaze.

"No she is *not*." Claire saw Nina surrounded by Cam, Derrington, and Josh. She was in the middle of their circle, twisting and twirling her arms in the air like a belly dancer, which was exactly what she looked like.

Nina was wearing black see-through harem pants, gold pumps, and a gold satin halter top. Her thick dark hair had been straightened and was pulled into a high ponytail. It looked like a horse's mane was growing out of her scalp.

"Why does Josh like her so much?" Alicia asked as she squeezed in between Claire and Massie. "She has the worst style."

"I know, and we have ah-mazing style," Massie said. "It makes no sense." Massie silently admired Alicia's turquoise halter dress and chunky salmon-colored necklace. The bright colors looked ah-mazing against her dark skin, and Massie felt the biting sting of envy. She wanted someone to think that she looked beautiful, and so far her parents were the only ones who had complimented her all night. And they didn't count.

Massie, Claire, and Alicia watched Nina dance with their guys for the rest of the song. They had no idea what to do next. A few schemes darted through Massie's brain, but nothing good enough to execute. They would make her look more desperate than Nina, and that was not what she was going for. Besides, that was what Layne, Meena, and Heather were for.

The three of them rushed the dance floor wearing nothing but potato sacks, chanting, "Nina the Obscena." But Nina didn't seem to mind. She started clapping along with Layne and trying to get her to join their circle of love.

"Oh my Gawd." Claire covered her smile with her hand. "Someone should be screaming, 'Layne is Insane.'"

"Mark the time and day." Massie grinned. "I just decided I officially like that girl. She's hilarious."

"What's with the potato sacks?" Alicia asked.

Massie and Claire shrugged.

Layne kept running away every time Nina pulled her closer, until eventually she left the dance floor in a huff.

"Layne," Claire yelled over the thumping beat of Eminem's "Just Lose It." She motioned for her friend to come over. Layne saw Claire and smiled. She hopped twice, then ran across the gym.

"I came as soon as you called," Layne panted. Meena and Heather pulled up behind her. "Did you want to join our protest?" She slid her orange faux-fur backpack off her shoulders and pulled out three more potato sacks. "I have enough for everyone."

Massie and Alicia jumped back as quickly as they could.

"No, that's okay," Claire said. "We just wanted to know what they were for."

Meena stepped forward. "They were my idea." She tucked a thick black corkscrew curl behind her ear. "They're meant to show people like Nina that you can still look beautiful in modest clothing."

"I got them from my dad's grocery store," Heather announced proudly.

"They should never have allowed boys at this dance." Layne shook her head. "They always bring out the worst in girls."

"You guys should change your names to the Sad Sacks." Massie's moment of affection for Layne was officially over.

"Hilarious," Layne mocked flatly. She stuffed the sacks

back in her bag and walked away. Meena and Heather followed her.

Alicia cracked up. Massie joined her when she noticed Derrington wipe his sweaty bangs away from his forehead and leave the dance floor. She wanted him to see that she could have fun without him. But he never even looked her way.

"Uh, 'bye, Layne," Claire called.

Layne lifted her hand over her head without turning around.

"Has anyone seen Kristen?" Mrs. Gregory said as she approached the girls. She was walking so quickly, Massie wondered if she'd be able to stop once she reached them or if she'd just smash into the wall.

"Uh, I think she's in the bathroom," Massie offered.

"As long as she's not hanging around that vixen on the dance floor," said Mrs. Gregory. "Where are that girl's parents?"

"Spain," Alicia replied.

Mrs. Gregory shook her head in disgust, then sat down with Dylan and Chris.

Massie felt a tingle in her stomach when she remembered that tonight was the night they were going to bring Nina down once and for all. She checked her diamond-encrusted Chanel watch. The big moment was only ten minutes away.

"Is everything set?" Massie asked Alicia.

"Given." Alicia swiped a red spot off her turquoise dress.

When she brushed her hand against it, it moved to Massie's shoulder.

"Ew, what is that?" Massie tried to wipe it off, but it moved to Claire's cheek. She lifted her hand as if she were about to smack a mosquito. "Kuh-laire, it's on your face."

Claire grabbed Massie's arm before she could do any damage. She turned her head and looked over her shoulder frantically, as if the mosquito had gotten away and she was trying to find it.

"There it is." Alicia pointed to the floor. "It's a laser light."

"Todd, where are you?" Claire shouted. Instantly he appeared, crawling out from under the table Dylan and Chris were sitting at. His tiny friend, Nathan, came out after him. They were both dressed in black cat suits.

"Please tell me those aren't my old dance clothes," Claire begged.

Tiny Nathan laughed, but it sounded more like a squeak.

"Claire, we have no time for banter." Todd lifted the rim of his black baseball cap, revealing a few strands of sweaty hair that had stuck to his forehead. "I am on a special mission. If we get caught at this dance, it could mean trouble for everyone." He was speaking from the side of his mouth. "So try to be cool."

He slipped Claire a CD case.

"What is this?" Claire said.

"Shhh," Todd and Nathan said at the same time. Then they giggled.

"It's a CD from you know who," he said.

"No way," Claire said. Her entire face lit up.

Massie felt her insides fill up with a heavy sadness. But she forced herself to half-smile, for Claire's sake.

"And this is for you." Todd reached into his pocket and pulled out a gold heart-shaped ring. It was oversized and made of plastic, but Massie didn't care. It fit perfectly, like it had been made just for her. She could feel herself smiling. Maybe her luck was about to turn. "Is this from Derrington?" she asked coyly.

"No." Todd sounded proud. "It's from me." He looked up at Massie with a loving smile.

Massie pulled off the ring and stuffed it down the collar of Todd's tight cat suit.

"Ouch. You're like a vicious animal!"

"Did you come all this way just to give me the CD?" Claire asked without taking her eyes off the front of the jewel case.

"Uh . . ." Todd looked nervously at Massie.

"He came because I made him." Massie grabbed him by the ear and pulled him toward her. "If you think he's getting away with spying on me, you're wrong."

Claire finally looked up. "Huh?"

"I figured he could help us with our revenge plan," Massie said. "And if he does a good job, I'll consider us even." She tugged his ear again and Todd moaned in pain.

"What does he have to do?" Claire's ah-nnoying protective instincts were obviously starting to kick in.

"Nothing too bad." Massie let go of Todd's ear and turned to face him. "All you have to do is offer to give Nina a foot massage. And while you do, Nathan will creep up behind you like a tiny mouse and steal her shoes."

"Then what?" Nathan squeaked.

"Then you will bring her shoes to me. I will make a few adjustments, and you will sneak them back to her."

"But her feet are all sweaty," Todd whined. "Look at her: she's dancing like a maniac."

"I never said this was going to be easy." Massie grinned. "Now go!" She slapped Todd on the butt and he took off toward the dance floor with Nathan trailing close behind.

Alicia started clapping, and Massie waited for Claire's reaction with an expectant smile on her face. She couldn't wait for Claire to jump up and down and congratulate her on thinking of another way to get Nina.

But all Claire said was, "I can't believe Cam didn't include a note."

"It looks like his playlist is the message," Alicia offered.

Claire looked at the CD cover one more time. "You're right."

"What does it say?" Massie figured that if she sounded interested, they'd never know how hurt she was that Claire wasn't excited about her latest revenge plan. And, more importantly, that Derrington hadn't sent anything for her.

Claire held the CD case in front of her face and read out loud.

"Sorry" Foxy Brown
"More Than Meets the Eye" The Bangles
"Don't Judge Me Bad" Monsieur Jeffrey Evans & the '68
Comeback
"Trouble Will Soon Be Over" Blind Willie Johnson
"True" Ryan Cabrera
"Great Big Kiss" New York Dolls
"Happy Valentine's Day" Outkast

"I have to find him. He totally wants to kiss tonight. The candy was right—it said **'Whatever Your Heart Desires,'** remember? I knew he'd send me a sign. I knew it." Claire hugged the CD and ran off to find Cam.

"It looks like she's chasing a little puppy." Alicia watched Claire zigzag frantically around the room, pushing innocent victims out of her way as she bobbed and weaved through clusters of people.

"She kind of is," Massie said.

Alicia giggled.

Massie felt bad insulting Cam, because she genuinely liked him. But acting mean helped her get rid of her pent-up Derrington anger. And she had a lot to get rid of.

"I've been waiting for like ten binutes for you to save us," Dylan whispered in Massie's ear.

"Huh?"

"Bissus Gregory has been sitting with us for the last twenty binutes. If she doesn't leave us alone, I'll never win dis bet." She blew her nose in a pink cocktail napkin, then casually dropped it on the floor.

"Is he really going to kiss you with that cold?" Massie asked.

"How are you going to breathe?" Alicia wondered.

Chris Plovert walked up and stood beside them.

"Uh, yeah, so I think I did okay on that bath test," Dylan said louder than she needed to. She obviously didn't want him to know what they were talking about.

"Uh, when you're done talking about math, we could check out my brother's new car," he said to Dylan.

"Uh, sure." Dylan twirled her hair and rocked back and forth on the heels of her gold wedge sandals. She looked casually over her shoulder. "But let's wait until Kristen's buther stops staring at us. She's giving me the creeps."

Chris rolled his eyes but agreed.

Massie was relieved. Obviously, Dylan was too nervous to be alone with Chris. Maybe she wasn't the only one with a kissing phobia after all.

"Let's go get some hot cider and cake," Dylan suggested, while biting her thumbnail, something she rarely did. "Then we can go to your brother's car." Dylan stared at Massie and Alicia with wide eyes, silently begging them to join her.

The four of them strolled over to the buffet table, but Dylan was the only one who grabbed a red, heart-shaped plastic plate. She tapped her finger against her chin while she scanned the selection, then she reached for a pink cupcake and six chocolate-covered strawberries. Massie,

Alicia, and Chris waited patiently while she searched for something salty to complement her sweets.

Josh Hotz was at the table, filling a plate with sprinkle cookies. When Alicia saw him, she applied a fresh coat of lip gloss and fluffed up her hair. Then she went back to acting like he didn't exist.

"Forget about the food." Chris's squinty eyes were fixed on Dylan. "Let's just go now."

Dylan twirled a lock of red hair around her finger and bit her bottom lip. She looked worried.

Alicia turned her back to Chris so he couldn't hear what she was saying. "Maybe you should go," she told Dylan. "Kristen has been gone for a while. You may want to pick up the pace." She gave her hair another quick fluff because Josh was now inches away.

"'Kay." Dylan pushed Alicia aside and spoke directly to Chris. She looked behind her and saw that Mrs. Gregory was busy talking to another one of the chaperones. "But we have to make a run for it so we can escape Kristen's bomb."

"I can't run." Chris knocked on his cast.

"Well, you better try," Dylan said. "Because Kristen's bomb is going to go off if she—"

Chris sighed and ran his fingers though his crunchy, overgelled hair.

Massie waved a pink cocktail napkin in front of Dylan's face. "Blow your nose," she instructed. "It looks moist."

Dylan handed her plate of food to Alicia, then blew into the napkin. She tossed it back to Massie.

"Ew." Massie jumped back and watched it land on the polished wood floor of the gym. She couldn't help laughing as she watched Dylan run in heels as Chris limped beside her.

"Where did Josh go?" Alicia's eyes searched the gym. "He was just here with a plateful of cookies."

"Dunno," Massie said. Derrington was chasing Nina around the dance floor, trying to lasso her with his red-and-blue-striped tie. He finally stopped when Todd and Tiny Nathan approached them. Derrington gave Todd a dirty look and then stumbled off the dance floor. Massie wished she had been standing closer so she could hear what Todd was saying, but whatever it was, it worked. Within seconds he had his hand on the small of Nina's back and was leading her toward an empty table. Tiny Nathan grabbed a red cloth napkin off a cookie-covered plate and wiped the chair before Nina sat down. Nina smiled with delight and patted the top of Todd's head. He giggled and then got down on his knees and pulled off her gold shoes, slowly, like a real Prince Charming would. Massie couldn't help smiling to herself: for a dork, Todd could be really smooth when he wanted to be.

"Come on, Nathan," Massie muttered to herself. "Grab the shoes and bring them to me. Come on. . . . Come on, little guy. . . . You can do it. . . . Yes!"

Nathan crept behind Nina's chair, pinched the heels of her shoes, and stuffed them down the back of his black tights. Then he crawled across the gym floor on his hands and knees. He stopped at Massie's heels.

"Gawd, you really took that whole Be-a-tiny-mouse thing

seriously, didn't you?" Massie said. He crinkled his nose and squeaked twice.

Massie reached into her handbag and pulled out a mini-saw.

"Ehmagod, where did you get that?" Alicia gasped.

"I kinda borrowed it from Claire's father. He's like, the only dad in Westchester who has his own toolbox." Massie crouched down so she could make eye contact with Tiny Nathan, who was still in mouse mode.

"Now crawl under a table and saw the heel halfway off of one of her shoes, but just halfway. When you're done, ditch the weapon and get the shoes back to Todd ASAP. Have him slip them back on Nina's feet, but try not to let her stand until she's called to the stage. Okay?"

Nathan squeaked and nodded. Then he quickly disappeared under a red tablecloth.

"Done," Massie sighed.

"Done," Alicia said.

"And done," Massie said.

Suddenly, the DJ lowered the volume on Kelly Clarkson's "Since U Been Gone," and Principal Burns began speaking from the small round stage they had built for the event.

"Is everyone having fun?" She was trying to sound enthusiastic, but it came out sounding more like she was making a statement than asking a question.

"I better go," Alicia said. "It's showtime."

"Are you all set?" Massie asked.

"I'm ready," Alicia replied. "But where's Claire?"

"Here." Claire ran up and stopped beside them. "Sorry 'bout that." She was out of breath.

"Did you kiss Cam?" Massie was hoping the answer was no. The idea of Claire having more experience than her in anything other than Keds and candy was unbearable.

Claire shook her head.

"Sorry to hear that," Massie lied.

"He ran away as soon as he saw me." Claire turned her head and wiped her eyes. "I'm sure he's laughing about all of this with Nina right now."

"Cheer up." Alicia patted Claire's shoulder. "Revenge is on its way. Wish me luck. It's time." She waved goodbye and for the first time in their friendship, Massie saw Alicia run. Her feet shuffled along the ground like she was doing a forward moonwalk, but to her credit, she was picking up speed.

"Good luck!" Massie and Claire shouted after her. Once Alicia was out of sight, they began pushing their way to the front of the stage. A lot was riding on the next five minutes and they didn't want to miss a thing. Massie's palms were starting to sweat. This was the first time she wasn't in complete control of a revenge plot, and she couldn't help wondering if Alicia had the chops to pull it off. If she didn't, they would probably face expulsion.

"It's time to present this year's Cupid Award," Principal Burns announced. The crowd started whooping and cheering. "Are we in position?" she asked one of her pudgy assistants by the gym door. The person must have told her they weren't, because Principal Burns closed her eyes and shook her head in frustration. Then she started rambling on about the rich history of the Cupid Award, probably to kill time.

Finally, Principal Burns got her long-awaited signal and stopped talking about the first couple to receive the Cupid Award back in 1958. A spotlight drew everyone's attention to the side doors of the gym. Harp music started playing and the doors burst open, giving way to a white horse-drawn carriage. Alicia was the only passenger. She looked like Cinderella as she smiled and waved to the envious crowd.

The driver pulled the reins and stopped the carriage a few feet from the stage.

"That jockey sucks," Massie whispered in Claire's ear. "I could have gotten that thing much closer."

Claire chuckled through her nose but didn't smile.

"You still thinking about Cam?" Massie said.

Claire shrugged.

"You need to flirt with someone new. It will totally take your mind off of him."

"Maybe."

The driver stepped off the horse and offered his white-gloved hand to Alicia. But she turned him down because her arms were filled with a chunky object covered in a white satin sheet. Everyone gasped when they saw it. They assumed it was the coveted Cupid Award.

"And here to announce this year's winning couple is Alicia Rivera." Principal Burns waved her arm. "OCD's fabulous newscaster."

"You're hot!" someone shouted. Everyone laughed and applauded. Alicia blew an air kiss and they cheered louder.

Principal Burns handed Alicia a gold envelope and was clearly expecting to relieve her of the cumbersome award. Her scrawny arms reached for it, and Massie felt like she was watching the whole thing in slow motion.

"Don't give it to her, Alicia. Don't give it to her." Massie hoped Alicia would pick up on her telepathy. "Don't give it to her. . . . *Yes!*" she said when Alicia ignored the gesture and managed to open the envelope with her teeth. A flurry of glitter fell out and almost choked Alicia. She spit a few times, but still had gold sparkles all over her lips.

The DJ played a drumroll off a sound effects CD while the lights dimmed. The white spotlight made it very hard for anyone to see anything other than the stage.

"The lucky couple that will be riding off into the parking lot in this beautiful carriage, holding each other and this year's Cupid Award is . . . "

Massie squeezed her eyes shut. She knew there was no way she could win, because she didn't even have a date, but she imagined her name being called anyway. Maybe they'd decided to change the rules this year, just for her. Or maybe this whole thing was a big practical joke for some kind of new MTV show and she'd really won. Maybe that was why Derrington had been acting like such a freak.

"For his amazing season on the soccer field and his ah-dorable kneecaps, Derrick Harrington," Alicia shouted into the mic.

Derrington jumped onto the stage and turned his back on his fans. Then he took off his red blazer, whipped it into the cheering crowd, and pulled down his khaki shorts so he could show off his famous butt-wiggle. Principal Burns stood in front of him until he pulled up his pants and turned around.

"You okay?" Claire asked Massie.

"Totally," Massie lied. "I'm over him. He's a child." She could still feel Claire looking at her. "I am, I swear."

Alicia reached under the satin cloth and pulled out the gold statue of Cupid shooting an arrow. She handed it to Derrington, who held it above his head like he had just won the World Cup.

"And now, for the girl you, the students of OCD and Briarwood Academy, chose to be his date," Alicia said.

Nina jumped out of her chair and pushed past Todd and Tiny Nathan. She started inching her way toward the stage.

"In the short time that she's been at OCD, she's managed to steal your hearts. . . ."

Nina smiled brightly.

"In fact, she's managed to steal everything that wasn't nailed down," Alicia said.

Then she whipped the satin cloth away and let it float to the ground. She was holding a long silver serving dish that was shaped like a giant boat. She had borrowed it from her mother's pantry.

Nina obviously hadn't picked up on Alicia's jab, because she was still waving and jumping up and down. Her boobs were fighting their way out of her satin halter top, and just as the left one was about to escape, her heel snapped and she fell flat on her perky little bubble butt. Her legs were splayed out in front of her, and the bright lights shone directly on her black harem pants.

Claire grabbed Massie's wrist and squeezed it tight. "Ew, her pants are totally see-though." She scanned the room to see if anyone else had noticed. "Look, everyone is pointing at her!"

"Ehmagod," Massie said.

Claire laughed for the first time all night. "If that doesn't turn the guys off, nothing will."

Nina waved her arm in the air, waiting for Derrington to help her up. But he showed no interest in Nina or what was happening to her. He was too busy shaking his butt and dancing around the stage, much to the delight of his soccer buddies.

Finally, Nina rolled over on her side and pushed herself up. The second she was standing, she fell again.

"That Tiny Nathan is no joke with a saw," Massie said.

The audience looked on with pity in their eyes. They covered their mouths and shook their heads, trying their hardest not to crack up at Nina's mortifying wipeout. But within seconds they lost all control, and suddenly the entire gym was filled with the sound of hysterical laughter.

Alicia was the only one who was oblivious to the audience's reaction. She was too focused on proceeding with her presentation ceremony. "So Nina," she continued, "we would like to honor you and the time you've spent at OCD by presenting you with the boatload of stuff you stole from everyone." Alicia dumped the contents of the silver boat onto Nina's head. Kristen's bike lock, Natalie's Chococat pencil case, Mrs. Beeline's red Montblanc, and Jessi Rowan's Kipling key chain all toppled down on Nina like the contents of an exploding piñata.

Nina looked up at her cousin; her thick dark eyebrows were scrunched as she searched Alicia's face for an explanation.

"Yes!" Massie threw her fist in the air. "We got her!" Massie searched Derrington's face for a reaction. "How do you like your sexy Spanish girlfriend now?"

"Hey, that's my key chain!" Jessi pushed her round glasses against her nose and made a mad dash for the stage. "Give me that!"

A mob of angry girls followed her, threatening to send Nina back to Spain with their fists.

Principal Burns opened her arms like a bird in flight and threw herself on top of Jessi. "Let's not use violence," she shouted as she wrapped her wiry arms around Jessi's shoulders and tried to pry her off of Nina. But Jessi refused to let go of Nina's ponytail. "Nina," Principal Burns yelled as she rode Jessi's back like a bucking bronco, "are these accusations true?"

Before Nina could respond, Principal Burns collapsed on

top of Jessi and the rest of the angry girls dog-piled them, trying to get closer to Nina. Mrs. Gregory and the other chaperones hurried toward the fray.

Finally, Jessi bit Principal Burns on the arm, which must have been a lot like biting into an undercooked chicken wing. Principal Burns squawked and Jessi broke free.

"Someone call Mr. Rivera!" Nina shouted as she kicked off her shoes and jumped to her feet. Strawberry and Kori rushed toward the deserted shoes and fought one another to claim them. "I need my lawyer." Nina jumped off the stage and ran as quickly as she could toward the exit. Jessi and the rest of the mob were only a few paces behind her.

"Puh-lease, like my dad would ever represent you!" Alicia shouted into the microphone. Then she looked up at the ceiling and shouted, "Release the photos!"

She snapped her fingers and hundreds of photographs fell from the sky like confetti. They were color copies of hideous Nina pictures from Alicia's scrapbook. Everyone stopped what they were doing and looked up in awe, like they were reveling in the first snowfall of the season.

"There are ten different hideous Nina photos," Alicia announced. "There's 'Braces and Zits'; 'Frizzy Afro'; 'Oops, My Pants Are Too Short'; 'Are Those Boobs or Blisters?'; 'Yes, My Sweatshirt Has Smiley Faces on It'; 'Help! These Boys Are Throwing Mud in My Face'; 'Even Dogs Think I'm Lame'; 'Granny Panties'; and my personal favorite, 'Flip-Flops and Sweat Socks.'"

Everyone raced around the room trying to catch as many photos as they could.

Massie could feel herself smiling. Everything was going perfectly. She stole a quick peek at Derrington, who just happened to be peeking at her. Massie felt her spine stiffen when their eyes met, and she quickly looked away.

"Uh, where's Nina?" Massie asked Claire. The sound of her own voice seemed unfamiliar and distant, like some mysterious thing inside of her had taken over and asked the question on her behalf. As if it knew Massie was still analyzing her exchange with Derrington and would remain frozen in time for a few seconds longer.

"There." Claire pointed to the gym doors.

Nina's arm was resting on the silver door handle like it was the only thing keeping her from collapsing. She extended her free hand and caught a falling photo, examined it closely, then buried her face in her shoulder.

"I wonder which one she's looking at," Massie asked Claire.

"I hope it's 'Frizzy Afro,'" Claire said. "It's the worst."

Nina's entire body started shaking.

"Yup, it's gotta be 'Frizzy Afro.'" Claire smiled. "That one would make me cry too."

"I'd lose it over 'Braces and Zits,'" Massie said.

"Collect all ten photos!" Alicia shouted like a carnival barker. "Trade with your friends. You can even—" But the girls' soccer coach grabbed the mic away from Alicia before she could finish her thought and yanked her off the stage.

Massie lifted her hands above her head and clapped for Alicia as she made her way toward them. Alicia bowed, then giggled.

Suddenly, Nina lifted her head in horror, as if she had just been told about a pop quiz. Jessi and her angry mob were standing right in front of her, cracking their knuckles. Nina shredded the picture she was holding and threw the scraps in Jessi's face. Just as Jessi was about to throw a punch, the fire alarm went off.

Everyone stopped what they were doing and looked around to find the fire. Instead they saw Josh Hotz running around in circles shouting, "Bomb! Bomb! Get out! She has a bomb." He was pointing at Kristen, who was standing at the back of the room with Kemp Hurley.

Nina pushed the gym doors open. She hurried through, then forced them to close in Jessi's face. Instead of following her, Jessi turned back toward the gym to check out Kristen's alleged bomb.

The guys on the soccer team jumped up on the stage so they could get a bird's-eye view of the action. It was obvious from their laughter and high fives that they thought Josh was just pulling another one of his fire alarm pranks. But the teachers and chaperones insisted that they evacuate anyway, just to be on the safe side.

The DJ started playing "The Roof Is on Fire" until Principal Burns ordered him to stop and everyone to leave at once. But no one did. The girls ambled over to their tables to get their handbags, while the guys raided the buffet table and stuffed as many cookies into their pockets as they possibly could.

"Let's go, people!" Principal Burns shouted over the microphone.

Fifteen minutes later, everyone was standing on the Great Lawn trying to figure out what was happening to Kristen Gregory in the back of the police car and why she would want to blow up the school.

"It still kinda feels like we're at the dance," Massie said as the blue and red lights of the police cars flashed across the crowd. Massie, Alicia, and Claire were on the cold grass under Massie's favorite oak tree.

Claire and Alicia giggled.

"I still don't understand why everyone is blaming Kristen," Alicia said.

"I heard that Josh heard Dylan talking about getting away from Kristen and her bomb." Massie shrugged.

"But why would he—?" Alicia was interrupted by Claire.

"I remember!" Massie shouted. "Dylan was telling Chris they had to get away from Kristen's *mom*, but her cold made it sound like *bomb*."

"And Josh was standing there for that," Alicia said. "I remember checking him out while they were talking."

"That's it!" Massie said.

Claire and Alicia obviously didn't know how to react, because both of their expressions froze halfway in between a laugh and a gasp.

"Ehmagod," Alicia wondered. "Should we say something?"

"Too late. I'm refe."

The girls rushed to Kristen's side and inspected her from head to toe to make sure she was okay.

"Did they hurt you?" Alicia asked.

"No, they just asked me a bunch of questions. Until my mom threatened to sue them. Now they're talking to Josh. They think he just pulled another prank. That kid is so dead to me."

"I think it's Dylan you should be mad at," Massie said.

"Why, did she kiss Chris Plovert?"

"Dunno yet," Massie replied. "Hey, has anyone seen Nina?"

"I heard she got taken away by campus security," Alicia offered.

Massie lifted her hand in the air and Claire and Alicia high-fived it.

"So, did you kiss Kemp?" Claire asked.

"Gawd, you are obsessed with kissing!" Massie said.

"I'm just curious."

"Bemya I did and bemya I didn't."

"What do you mean, 'maybe'?" Claire asked. "Did you or not?"

Kristen shrugged and smiled.

"Where have you guys been?" Dylan huffed. "I've been looking all over for you. We should have some sort of beeting spot in case of emergency evacuations."

"We do," Massie said. "This is it."

"Oh yeah, right. Sorry. I think my feber is coming back."

She wiped the thin layer of sweat off her forehead.

"So, where were you?" Kristen asked Dylan, pressing for information.

"In the back of Chris's car. Where were you?"

"In the janitor's closet with Kemp."

"So who won the bet?" Claire asked.

"Obsessed," Massie said.

"I just want to know that at least one of us got kissed at this stupid dance." Claire pulled a chunk of grass out of the ground and threw it at her own feet.

"Where's Deena?" Dylan asked. "I feel like she should be the first to doh."

Massie searched Dylan's face for clues to see if she had really kissed Chris or if she was just stalling. But it was hard to tell. She just looked sick.

"Nina was taken away by security," Alicia said.

"Doh way," Dylan said. "Why?"

"Your precious Deena is a criminal and a designer imposter, that's why," Massie said. "She stole those boots from her sisters. So even if you won the bet, you couldn't keep them."

"I knew it!" Kristen obviously lied. She pulled her dowdy clothes out of her green Club Monaco bag and quickly started layering them over the Diane von Furstenberg beaded silk chiffon dress Massie had lent her. "Anyway, I'm glad that's over."

"What does that bean?" Dylan asked. "Does that bean you lost?"

"Did you?" Kristen asked.

"Did you?"

"Did you?"

"I asked you first," Dylan said.

"Well, we were getting really close to kissing, but the fire alarm went off and we had to leave," Kristen said as she pulled her white knit teddy bear turtleneck over her head. "What about you?"

"Same." Dylan looked relieved.

"But you were outside, in a car," Massie piped in.

"I know, but what if it had been a car bomb?" Dylan said.

Everyone started cracking up, and Massie felt light and giddy for the first time in weeks. Now that Nina was gone, Kristen and Dylan could stop acting like sex-starved aliens. They were back. And that felt almost as good as winning the Cupid Award. . . . Almost.

┌ ─ ┐
│   │
│   BRIARWOOD ACADEMY   │
│   THE FINALS   │
│   Saturday, February 14th   │
│   1:17 P.M.   │
│   │
└ ─ ┘

Massie wrapped her new green-and-gold-striped scarf around her head so that Derrington would have a better chance of seeing it from the soccer field. Wearing Grayson's team colors to the finals game instead of Briarwood's was the least Massie could do to repay him for breaking her heart and depriving her of the Cupid Award.

It wasn't like she wanted to sit in the freezing cold on an overcast Saturday afternoon and cheer for a bunch of guys who'd spent the last two weeks trying to humiliate her and her friends. But of course, her mother had forced her to go, to support Todd and his ah-nnoying tuba. When was someone going to support *her*?

"Massie, no." Claire stopped walking down the concrete stadium steps and started heading back up to the top.

"What is your problem?" Massie asked.

"I'm not sitting that close to the field. What if Cam sees me?"

"That's the whole idea." Massie pinched Claire's cheeks to give her pale skin a burst of color. "Let him see what a good time you're having without him."

"What if he thinks I'm stalking him?"

"Just look away if he looks at you and make sure you're smiling," Massie advised. "Always look like you're having fun."

Claire sighed. "I can't believe I'll never get my kiss."

"You will," Massie assured her. "It just may not be from Cam."

Claire lowered her big blue eyes and Massie searched for something more positive to say. She walked up two steps to meet Claire and then put an arm around her.

"Look at all of the guys out there. Just pick someone else. Pretend we're here to shop for boys. That's what I'm doing. The spring dance is right around the corner, and I am not going alone again."

"I guess that could be kinda fun." Claire looked into Massie's eyes.

"Totally," Massie said. "Remember, keep smiling. We have to show them that they can't get to us."

"'Kay." Claire forced herself to grin before she followed Massie down the steps toward their friends.

"Sorry we're late," Massie said as she slid past Kristen and Alicia. They were seated in the front row, right behind the Briarwood locker room. "We had to pack up Claire's stuff because the movers are coming today."

"Are you excited to move into your new house?" Kristen asked as Claire climbed over her knees to get to her seat.

"I'm excited that I don't have to sleep in Massie's bathtub anymore." Claire sat down.

Alicia and Kristen looked at Massie to see if Claire was joking, but Massie kept her eyes focused on the game, pretending not to notice. Derrington was standing in the goalie net, biting his thumbnail and watching the ball.

"What are you wearing?" Kristen asked Massie. She looked disgusted.

"I was just about to ask you the same thing," Massie fired back. Kristen was dressed in head-to-toe Briarwood Tomahawks gear again. If her hair had still been long, her look might have passed for tomboy chic, but there weren't any cute wispy pieces of blond hair peeking out of her cap, so she looked like one of the players.

"At least I'm showing a little team spirit. You look like you're rooting for the other team."

"I am." Massie leaned back and drenched her lips in a thick, delicious coat of Caramel Fudge Sundae, her newest arrival from Glossip Girl. She handed the tube to Claire and made her apply a coat.

Kristen grunted and folded her arms across her chest. She had nothing more to say.

"That smells ah-mazing," Alicia said to Massie.

"I know," Massie said. "They've started sending good flavors again."

"Maybe your luck is changing." Claire handed the tube back to Massie.

"Doesn't feel like it," Massie said just as Derrington saved a goal. The whole crowd jumped to its feet and cheered for him. Massie rolled her eyes. "See."

"A saved goal is a good thing." Kristen looked down at Massie, who was the only one in the crowd still sitting.

"I wish he'd gotten hit in the face instead."

They all looked at her in horror. "What?" Massie asked innocently. She ran her finger along the purple rhinestones of her *M* brooch that was attached to her white Michael Kors pea coat.

"You should take that back," Kristen said.

But Massie refused to apologize. After all, Derrington had hurt her first.

"So, did Nina ever make it home last night?" Massie changed the subject. She was tired of them looking at her like she was a serial killer.

"By the time I came home, her bags were packed and her plane ticket was already booked." Alicia chuckled. "We drove her to the airport this morning. And her angry sisters will be picking her up when she lands."

"Gone," Massie said.

"Gone," Alicia said.

"And gone," Claire said. The girls giggled and high-fived each other.

Just then Cam looked toward the bleachers. He noticed Claire and smiled shyly. She looked away.

"Nice move," Massie nodded. "That was perfect."

"Cool." Claire's mouth smiled but her eyes didn't.

"Now wave at another player when he's looking," Massie said.

Just then, Josh Hotz looked their way and Claire waved at him. Josh smiled and waved back.

"Nice." Massie was impressed by Claire's confidence around boys.

"Great." Alicia rolled her eyes. "Now that Nina's gone, why don't you go for him?" she said to Claire. "Gawd knows he doesn't like me."

"Really?" Claire said. "You're over him?"

"Oh, sure. Why not?" Alicia threw her hands in the air.

Claire tightened the strings on the hood of her blue coat until it pinched her face and squished her eyebrows together.

"You two would be perfect together," Alicia said. "He loves Kenny from *South Park*."

Claire pushed the hood off her head and rolled her eyes.

"Look," Massie said. "Josh keeps looking at you now. My advice worked."

"Oh, how great for you both." Alicia rolled her eyes again.

"Who needs Nina's advice when we have Massie?" Kristen said.

"I've been trying to tell you and Dylan that for weeks," Massie said.

"By the way, where *is* Lydan?" Kristen asked.

"She's on major bed rest." Massie flipped open her phone. "Look at the text message she sent me."

DYLAN: Can't go 2 the game. My throat is on fire. I can't even eat. How great is that? I feel lighter already. Have fun. ☺

"She is so not fat," Alicia said. "I swear she can be so ah—"

A loud *pop* came from the field and drew their attention back to the game. As soon as Massie saw what had happened, she covered her mouth with her hands and immediately turned away from Kristen.

"Derrington just got tagged in the face!" Kristen jumped out of her seat to get a closer look. He was lying on his back in front of the goalie net, rubbing his nose and writhing in pain. "You willed it," she said to Massie. "You did this."

"I did not," Massie said, wondering if maybe she really had.

"Did too!" Kristen shouted. "Now we're going to lose and it's your fault! You're like some sort of crazy witch."

Massie held her palm in front of Kristen's face. "Calm down, sir."

"Witch." Kristen pulled her hat over her boy cut.

"Male," Massie shot back.

"Witch."

"Male."

Two referees carried Derrington off the field and sat him down on the bench. He was rocking back and forth, but it was clear he was going to survive.

"Hey, you!" the Briarwood coach shouted. "Hey, number 22!" He was jumping up and down and waving.

"Kristen, I think he's talking to you," Alicia said.

"Huh?"

"What are you doing up there?" he shouted. "Get down here! We need you."

"No way," Kristen muttered under her breath. "That jerk thinks I'm a dude."

"Don't be upset. I think it's the outfit, not the hair." Massie suddenly felt bad for calling Kristen a male. "But you *are* wearing their uniform. You can't take it personally."

"Upset?" Kristen said. "I'm stoked!" She dropped her pink-and-black velvet Juicy Couture bowling bag on Massie's lap. "Watch this for me."

"Are you serious?" Massie asked.

"Totally." Kristen winked. "It's a guy thing. You wouldn't understand." She hopped over the fence and ran onto the field, her arms punching the cold air above her head. "I love my haircut!" she shouted back at her friends.

The crowd exploded when they saw her. Even Massie was on her feet now. Number 14 stepped into the net and Kristen took his place on the field. This game was finally getting interesting.

When the horn signaled halftime, Grayson Academy was winning, 1–0. Number 17 scored a goal despite Kristen's impressive attempt to stop him. But, as the announcer said, "They don't call him Lightning Legs for nothing."

The halftime show began and Massie couldn't help giggling when she saw Todd march across the field. The chin strap on his hat was pressing down on his nose, and he kept waving his tuba the wrong way and hitting the guys next to him.

"What a doof," Claire said.

"Speaking of doofs . . ." Massie checked the display on her vibrating phone. "Derrington just sent me a text message." Her voice was surprisingly calm.

"Oh my Gawd, what does it say?" Claire was ten times more excited than Massie. "Is he with Cam?"

Massie bit her bottom lip, squinted, and shook her head.

"Sorry. I'll stop."

"Thank you," Massie said as she dropped her phone back in her coat pocket.

"Aren't you going to read it?" Alicia said.

"No," Massie said. "We're done."

"You're so strong," Claire said. Alicia nodded in agreement.

The truth was, Massie was too afraid of what the message might say. What if Derrington just needed someone's phone number or the name of a good hairdresser? Then she'd be even more embarrassed and hurt than she already was, and she didn't want anyone to witness that. She would have to wait until she got home.

Suddenly, Alicia began giggling uncontrollably.

"What's so funny?" Massie asked.

But Alicia was too busy scrolling through Massie's cell phone to answer, "'Massie, meet me behind the visitors' bleachers ASAP,'" Alicia read.

Massie's heart started pounding and her hands became clammy. She couldn't tell if she was reacting to Derrington's message or the fact that Alicia had swiped her phone and read it without her permission. All she knew for sure was that she wanted to punch Alicia and hug her at the same time.

"What can I say?" Alicia shrugged. "I guess stealing runs in my family."

"Lemme see that." Massie grabbed the phone. Claire leaned in to get a closer look. They read the message again.

"You have to go. We need answers."

"I say make him suffer," Alicia said. "He doesn't deserve you."

Massie had no idea what to do next. She agreed with both of them.

"Where are the hearts?" she asked Claire.

"Gone. I finished them ages ago. But they don't work anyway."

The sound of the marching band suddenly seemed louder to Massie, like it was purposely trying to distract her from making the right decision. It was impossible to think clearly, especially with Alicia and Claire staring at her.

"I know," Claire said. "I'll flip a coin. Heads you go, tails you don't."

"'Kay," Massie agreed.

Claire tossed the quarter. They watched it hang in the air, then tumble back down into Claire's open palm.

"Come on, tails," Alicia said.

Don't listen to her, Massie silently begged the Coin Gawds.

When the coin landed, Claire smacked her free hand over it.

"Well?" Massie and Alicia looked at Claire encouragingly.

Claire peeked under her hand. "Heads." She quickly stuffed the quarter in her back pocket.

Massie could tell Claire was lying, because her face turned bright red and she lowered her eyes to the pavement.

"Well, I guess I have to go." Massie stood up. "How do I look?" She took off her Grayson scarf and casually dropped it in Claire's lap.

"Perfect, as usual," Alicia assured her.

"Good answer." Massie smiled and waved goodbye. Then she turned and ran up the stairs, two at a time.

She stopped a few feet short of the visitors' bleachers to check her hair and makeup. Her cheeks were naturally rosy from the cold, and her hair was shiny and full—not a frizz to be found. *Break his heart,* she told herself as she clicked her Chanel compact shut. *It's showtime.*

The grass was stiff with frost, and it crunched under Massie's feet as she walked under the metal bleachers to their meeting spot. She could feel her stomach locking with every step she took. Did she look as nervous as she felt? What did he want? Would she still think he was cute now that his nose was all busted up?

"Mass?" he mumbled.

She felt her heart drop when she saw him. It seemed like ages since she'd been allowed to openly look at his face. He was better looking than she remembered, even with the swollen purple nose. His shaggy blond hair was messy in a good way, and his cheeks were rosy from the cold. The expression in his twinkling brown eyes was sweet and kind, nothing like the mischievous butt-shaking, shorts-wearing clown the rest of the school saw. Massie immediately tried to harden her eyes so Derrington wouldn't know what she was thinking.

"Do I look like Bozo?" He touched his nose lightly. It was so swollen, his full lips seemed tiny.

"You wish," Massie said.

Derrington chuckled and then held his jaw. "Ow."

Massie clenched her teeth to stop herself from smiling. She didn't want Derrington to know she was happy he'd laughed at her joke.

The crowd started booing. Massie assumed Grayson had scored another goal.

Derrington looked down at his brown Pumas and rubbed his forehead until his sweaty bangs stuck straight up in the air.

Why did she find him so ah-dorable? He was actually kind of dirty.

"It wasn't even worth it." Derrington lifted his hands toward his chest and yanked on the straps of his backpack.

Massie had no idea what he was talking about.

When she didn't respond, he raised his eyes without lifting his head and looked at her.

"What?" Massie knew she sounded impatient but didn't care. She had every right to. "What wasn't worth it?"

"The Spanish soccer spell," Derrington said flatly, as if Massie should have known exactly what he was talking about.

"Are you poor?" Massie asked.

"No," Derrington said. "Why?"

"Because you're not making any cents," Massie said.

Derrington grabbed his jaw again when he smiled.

"You know, the spell Nina put on me, Cam, and Josh before the game," he explained.

Massie shook her head.

"We couldn't talk to our . . . . Well, you know, we couldn't talk to you guys before the game. If we did, we'd lose the finals. If we stayed away from you, we'd win. It's the same spell Becks uses."

"Huh?" was all Massie could say. Her brain was trying to catch up to his mouth.

"Apparently David Beckham doesn't talk to Posh Spice for weeks before a big game. But it works for him. It totally didn't work for us. Grayson is kicking our butts." He paused. "And my face."

"You actually bought that?" Massie wasn't sure whether she wanted to hug Derrington or smack him for being so stupid.

"What do you mean?" Derrington asked. "Nina said you, Claire, and Alicia were all for it."

"Oh yeah. We were. You know, if it works for Beckham, then . . ." Massie let her voice trail off. There was nothing left to say. Everything suddenly made sense.

"Except it didn't work for *us*," Derrington mumbled. His brown eyes looked childlike and sad. "Not only are we losing the game, but I'll never get the MVP pin now that I've been taken out.

"And we couldn't go to the dance together." Massie couldn't resist.

"Yeah," Derrington said. "That was the worst part."

That was all he needed to say. Massie's insides started to tingle, like an electrical current was running through her veins making her feel alive and squirmy at the same time.

"At least you won the Cupid Award."

"Oh yeah." Derrington slid his backpack off his shoulder and let it fall to the ground. "I almost forgot." He reached inside and pulled out the gold statue. "This belongs to you."

"Are you serious?"

"Yeah."

"Thanks." Massie grabbed the cold statue from his warm hands. Then her smile faded.

"What's wrong?"

"Nothing. It's just that . . . well, no one will know I have it. So it's not like I really won it."

"You'll know." Derrington put his hand on his heart. "Isn't that enough?"

"It would be if this was the end of a cheesy Disney movie," Massie said.

Derrington chuckled with his mouth closed and Massie could tell he was hurt.

"OMG, I'm totally kidding," she lied. "Of course it's enough." She reached for the *M* brooch on her lapel and unpinned it. Then she leaned in toward Derrington and grabbed him by his soccer jersey. It was wet with sweat, but she pinned it on him anyway.

"What's this?" Derrington pulled his shirt away from his chest and looked down at the brooch.

"It's your MVP pin. Just without the V or the P. Its way cuter than the boring silver ones your coach gives out."

"Thanks." Derrington managed to smile without holding his face. "I'll wear it forever."

"Promise?" Massie asked.

"Promise," Derrington said.

And she believed him.

There was a spilt second between the time when their faces met and their lips actually touched, during which Claire was strangely aware of her thoughts.

Should I tilt my head first and then close my eyes? Or close, then tilt? How will Massie react when she finds out? How many times will I be asked to retell this story? Will anyone believe me? What are the chances of his lips tasting like grape Big League Chew? Am I supposed to stick my tongue out now? What about now? What about—?

Suddenly the questions fell away and Claire's entire body felt like it was filling up with hot maple syrup. She was actually pressing her lips against his. It was happening. It was totally happening.

So what if they weren't at a Valentine's Day dance. So what if he was shorter. So what if his armpits smelled like sour cream 'n' onion chips because he'd just played soccer for two hours. *I am getting my first kiss,* she told herself as his wet tongue tried to poke through her closed mouth. *Nothing else matters.*

But that wasn't entirely true.

Suddenly, Claire heard the sound of footsteps crunching on the frozen grass. She pulled away so fast, her eyes were still closed. When she opened them, she found herself staring at Cam, just like the hearts said.

"What are you doing?" he asked. His expression was blank, his tone flat. His voice reminded Claire of the AOL "You've Got Mail" guy.

"Uh . . ." was all Claire could say.

"Hey, Cam," said Josh Hotz. He wiped his lips and stuffed his hands in the pockets of his navy sweats.

"So much for the Spanish soccer spell." Cam looked at his Adidas cleats. Then he sighed. "And my friends." He turned his back on Claire and Josh and shuffled away slowly, kicking up patches of grass with every step he took.

"Cam, wait!" Claire shouted after him. "What soccer spell? What are you talking about?"

He started running, just like he had during the Love Struck dash. Only this time Claire understood why.